FEDDOR

He who doesn't read
Is equivalent to he who can not read.
Reading is truly fundamental.

THE ULTIMATE POLITICIAN

As you read this literary work, I query you (the reader) to envision the attached information as that of a fascinating movie. A thriller, a suspense; or maybe even a horror of sorts. Yet, think realistically of this work in the realm of your own (one's) personal life; and how all of this applies directly to you. For it truly does. And as you read, connect the dots of information revealed both literally and subliminally (to your inner Spirit Man), and assess what one must accurately do; and then do-so accordingly.

A brief note from the author.
None of the attached information is a personal attack on ANYONE Personally, or NO GROUP, nor Institution and (nor) Organization.
It is all relevant information shared that ALL are privy (privied) to.
For this is not a campaign, yet it (IS) a lifestyle of propriety.

Enjoy

FEDDOR

THE ULTIMATE POLITICIAN

FEDDOR
The Ultimate Politician

THE ULTIMATE POLITICIAN

Kingdom vs Democracy

To understand these two (2) completely different forms of Country's Style/Governments, let's paraphrase what each of these two (2) entities represents.

A Kingdom has a King (Queen) as its Head, over All its citizens of the Land.

And when a Kingdom takes over a new terrain, The King is that Sovereign Power Authority of Governmental Influence over it's (new) Territory; impacting it with The Sovereign's Intent.

A Democracy has elected officials, voted in by its Citizens, this includes the Office of the President; who stands as Head.

In a Kingdom, the King makes all of its Laws; and Rules. Though He (She) has a group of people on a panel, overseeing and discussing these Laws, Rules or Decrees, and Amendments, yet, He - The Sovereign (She) says "Yay or Nay"; to what these rules of the Land Shall Be. Thus, Hence and

Therefore, everything is enforced; via WHAT saith the King (Queen).

In a Democracy, the Laws and Rules of the land are usually ushered in via votes; from its Citizens. The citizens (also) voted in the cabinet members to represent them, their ideas and needs, for what they perceive to be for a better quality of life for their Community, their Families; and so forth. In a Democracy voting counts for everything, and is ever changing, due to (updated) environmental and strong Media Influence; of societal (ever changing) diversified demographics.

Often times with Kingdom's, they would seek additional territories; and take over other lands When this occurs and the land is taken over, they set up what is known as the process of "COLONIZATION" in that new land territory.
The King then would send his Most Important designated person into that new territory, and He is the "Governor".
The Governor's responsibility is to get that new territory to mirror exactly the Kingdom that the King possesses. Everything is to be done

accordingly, as to how things are done in the Kingdom.

All the Laws, Rules, Decrees, and Percepts from the Kingdom are instilled, enacted and enforced; in this new territory. And if the people speak a different language, they are to be stripped of their language, and now acquire the new language; of the Kingdom. Furthermore if the people have Cultures and Customs that they possessed Prior, they are to be taken away, and thus given this new culture of the Kingdom, and learn all things Anew, for the Kingdom is the new owner of this territory; and old WAYS are abolished.

And with the Kingdom now possessing this land, and the Governor instilling all the forms of Laws, Languages, Customs and &c., from the Kingdom, the King of this land and the Kingdom is now responsible for Everything Upon This Land; along with its newly acquired Citizens.

Therefore, the Kingdom is responsible for the Citizens, their Well-being, and their Lifestyle; as long as it (they) conforms to the Precepts of the Kingdom.

In a Democracy, they usually have independent States forming a Federation; making up the conglomerate of the lands. And in each State, the most important and highest position of that state is that of the Governor, yet, he is a voted in (elected) official; and he (too) Can be voted out.

Thus, on this note let's briefly touch base on Slavery, (the Enslavement of Africans and African Americans), the Indentured Servitude; and the Assisted Migration Penance - of the (Europeans). These institutions were started while under a Kingdom, prior to defection taking place, especially from here in the States, and other countries abroad, thus, causing these (all mentioned enslaved Persons, both Africans and Europeans) identities are/were stripped; from All these Bound individuals. Those Bound groups coming from Europe were informed, "If you shall live, never Return." As for the African, it was understood, "You shall Surely Die." You can read independently books on this subject matter for further enhancement, by this self same author "Isznen Feddor":
The Potomac at Mount Vernon,
Lil's Daughter Freilina Goldie and Other Stories, & The Brilliance.

FEDDOR

The Governor

The Most Important person in any newly acquired territory is
"The GOVERNOR."
This fact stands True, regardless if it is for a Kingdom; or a Federation of States.
The Governor will have his own Mansion, in each of these locations; as part of his benefits.
It is important to understand the relationship of the Governor, and that of whom he represents (If); under a Kingdom. For the Governor states (verbalizes) everything dictated to him from the King. For the Governor is his designated Ambassador/Representative, and therefore; he has No Opinion of his own. He is to ONLY reiterate all of the King's mandates, laws and decrees; and enforces Everything Exactly as the King has instructed.
If (ever) the Governor is asked by anyone in this new territory to give (his personal) opinion, his immediate answer is; "I have no opinion of My Own. I speak ONLY that which the King requests and insists".

FEDDOR

And if the people in that society, (the citizens) ask the Governor (of that Kingdom) if he could mediate, and possibly make some amendments or changes - and or present to the King, the Governor shall advise; "Absolutely Not. This is what the King has set forth, and this is how it shall be. And in doing so, you shall receive full benefits of Citizenship, along with all its Entitlement, of what's Deemed to you; from the King - over this Land."

Whereas, the Governor in a Democracy; represents the People. Therefore, he is a Mediator. For he sends requests to the President and its Government, from the people. And the President will send responses, via the Governor, back to the Citizens of that designated State, and from there Laws, Bills, and or Amendments; are adhered to. Under a Federation of States, and the Governor is a mediator. There is much back and forth-ness of voting, and discussions between the People, the Governor, Congress, and the President; and going through the legal channels of policy; (in) getting a Bill - passed into a Law.

The Governor in both of these instances are Most Valuable…

THE ULTIMATE POLITICIAN

FEDDOR
Politicians and Campaigning

When a Politician decides to run for office, or even
take office, and or maintain his/her seat In-office;
campaigning is key. He/she puts forth all of their
desires (Ideas and Beliefs), of things to be done;
and changes to be made.   And, it is at this time
that the people from the public understand this
politician's ideology; and what they believe in. And
if it sizes up to the people's beliefs and their
ideology, usually they are voted upon. This is also
a very dangerous time - often for that politician,
because you have some people in society who
don't like politicians, their ideology, and any form of
campaigning, and they would attempt to
assassinate them; or cause harm (physically) upon
them. Let alone, other politicians perform smear
campaigns against that rival person; with slander.
Keep in mind, Slander is truth spoken about
someone; that would harm them irreparably.

Church & State

It is understood that both Church and State were separated as a law in 1905, keeping these two (2) entities apart. Yet, the question remains as to why this is somewhat enforced, when many, if not most of the laws with the States, actually stem (derived); from the Church.

Most of the Laws on the books are structured according to the laws set forth from the original Ten Commandments, dating back to "BC". And then, these Laws were passed down to the various churches; starting as early as the First Century "AD".

Most of the Magistrates enforce these same Laws, as of today.

Incidentally, most of the Magistrates (Chief Justices) on the high Court, the Supreme Court here in the States, are representatives from Higher Learned Jesuit Institutions, from the Church; over the Land.

It is understood and expected, that these same Magistrates (Chief Justices) enforcing these laws are to be neutral (impartial), without an opinion, yet, they are heavily & highly educated from this Church's influence (of indoctrination) in their learning; thus shaping and regulating their thinking. Though they are to be opinion free, yet, there is still much indoctrination, causing one to perceive that the judgment (of these Justices); might be already tainted & clouded.

So again, the question comes to mind; is there really a separation of church and state. I personally have no problem with the Church's influence over the State. Actually, I prefer it. For it appears that many problems have come into existence, where the separation of the Church influence over the State - has come into play, an example of this is - taking Prayer out of the Public Schools, or - the allowance of gender neutral bathrooms; and &c.

One can study independently on this subject matter. It is a very hot and sensitive topic, for some much-needed dialogue, along with the ideology of your local Politicians; and Congressman's. For on this topic alone, it is an ever pressing and changing one; at Present.

THAT SAID....

Let's now discuss this literary work.

Of all that was already mentioned, thus far, on the previous pages; leads up to the topic of this concerto (composition).

The Ultimate Politician.

Who was The Ultimate Politician?
The only true Candidate and Politician we must recognize and categorize, of all that was said in this configuration thus far, leads us to understand; this person is none other than: JESUS "The CHRIST" Yeshua. God In the Flesh. Emmanuel, God amongst us.

For Jesus Christ is known as the Unction of days. He is born of blood - first, with no genealogy. He is not a created being, he was born. Birthed into this Human Experience. For HE came down from Heaven for us, the Unction of Days..
For Christ is known as the Angel of the Lord. And he is the only one that can be worshiped. For he's

not an angel, he's God; that has come down in the Flesh.

Let's break this all down, to understand how this all has come about. One can independently obtain previous work by this author, "Posterity" to go into Great Lengths of details; of how this has come about. Yet, in order for one to understand who Jesus truly is, and what he did in coming to earth, one must understand; All that Adam lost….
Jesus sole purpose for coming here was to restore man back to being a Son, (Restoration) to be placed back BETTER than Before, and to his rightful Position; of Dominion over Earth. For Adam TREASONOUSLY relinquished his position, as a Son. In addition, he FELL from DOMINION over ALL the Earth and EVERYTHING WITHIN, relinquishing this over to the adversary (the devil). He (Adam) should have been put to death on the spot. Because all treasonous acts (throughout History), are usually met with Death. But God (Our Heavenly Father) was merciful, and spared him. And he (Immediately) had restoration, placed into motion. For he brought forth the second Adam, being himself, coming in the Flesh; for (Himself) to be the ultimate sacrificial lamb - for Man.

Therefore, it is incumbent for one to truly understand Kingdom lifestyle, and to possess; a Kingdom mindset. For it is this reason we commenced this composition, briefly going into the differences between a Kingdom; and a Democracy.

God's (Our Heavenly Father) only intent Was to make (duplicate), his Heavenly Kingdom; here on Earth. For God never intended to come to Earth and inhabit it for himself. He's in Heaven, for this is his dwelling. Nor has God intended for man to go (come) to Heaven. For this is a religious concept (and mindset), that he has no intent on having done (happen). Man is to inhabit Earth forever. His spirit will (that is). God made Earth for man. His sons, (incorporate both sons and daughters). For a spirit has no gender. Our spirits (those of us who are Sons of God), will inhabit this Earth - Forever.

Keep in mind, a Kingdom is a Government's influence over its territory, impacting it with its Sovereign's (God - Our Heavenly Father), the King of ALL of this (Man on Earth); Intent.

FEDDOR

God never wanted servants of man, he ONLY wants Son's….
And when I say Son's, I'm incorporating both sons and daughters; as one.
God already has servants. His servants are the Angels, (created creatures) up in heaven with him. He has some that sing to him, and some that fight for him, some that do various tasks, and he has billions of them (Angels), that are assigned to us here on Earth, to be our servants; and to yield to us whatever we ask. Because God (Our Heavenly Father), has already done everything for us, therefore, he has assigned his angels unto us, to yield to us whatsoever we want; when asked. So understand, these are his servants that tend to him; and us. Therefore, Our Heavenly Father doesn't want servants of us - here upon earth; he ONLY wants Son's.
For Man is NOT a created creature (such as the angels), he is born of flesh and blood - BEING. And we are after the image of God, image meaning characteristics and character; Sonship MINDSET.

Man IS a SON...............

We (Man) are here on Earth as Dignitaries. Ambassadors. Representatives of Our Heavenly Father's Kingdom. We are his sons, and we are his Representatives; here on Earth. And we are to speak as the Father does. For this makes him so proud of us, when we act like him. He loves this… He says, "Look at my Boy, he talks and acts like me. Because he knows his Authority, and his Position". This truly makes him so Proud. For this reason, he has given us his written word, that we are to live by the Holy Bible; which is our Constitution. Every country has a Constitution and or Precepts, and standards; for its citizens of that country - to abide by. So does Our Heavenly Father. It's our Holy Bible. It is our Constitution of our LEGAL Rights, and our Entitlement of Things, and what Belongs to us (Son's). Therefore, we are Never to suffer, nor Lack, for he is Our Heavenly Father; Our Provider (El Elyon & Jehovah Jireh). For He owns everything and lacks nothing, and possesses NO sickness; and we are Him on Earth.

When Jesus (Yeshua, God in the flesh), began being recognized here upon earth, it was after he was baptized; by John the Baptist (his cousin). For John the Baptist welcomed Christ presence into existence to the community, as the Messiah, and shortly thereafter John the Baptist (was arrested & beheaded, reluctantly by Herod) after he granted any request from his daughter, of which she turned to her mother, and the mother demanded this beheading; by way of the daughter - request. And from there, Christ (Yeshua), at age 30 - began his mission upon earth, for the next 3&1/2 years, to finalize the restoration process of man; back to his rightful position.

From that point on, Christ taught (spoke openly), one thing; and one thing ONLY.   Let me say it again. One thing, and one thing only, THE KINGDOM.

He spoke in parables, always to the masses; about the Kingdom of God.

For the Kingdom of God is like a man that found a pearl, in the ground….

For the Kingdom of God is like a farmer who planted wheat…

For the Kingdom of God is like that of a mustard seed… and &c.

Yet, be it understood, Christ NEVER taught, spoke about, nor preached; "WORSHIP ME".

Christ's opening statement, when he begins speaking in the synagogue, and to the public "seek ye first the kingdom of God and his righteousness; and all these things are (automatically) added". And Christ mentions this immediately, after he said "repent" (change your Thinking/Mindset); for the Kingdom of God has ARRIVED.

And of course, the Jewish High Priests, and all the high-minded religious leaders, didn't like this doctrine; he was saying. And they thought this was pompous of him, arrogant, and blasphemous. For this is the son of both Joseph and Mary, yet, he's talking in public, Advising the crowds that the Kingdom of God has arrived in him; being present upon Earth. And these same High Priests, murmured heavily amongst each other (against him), because Christ had never been in any of their discipleship nor tutelage; in learning.

And all the while speaking to the masses, Christ never taught nor spoke about - being born again. This was mentioned once, and once only by him, when he spoke privately and directly to Nicodemus, the Head High Priest; and it was a metaphor. Other than this, he never mentioned

Born Again; ever again. For this was NOT the Good News he brought. The Good News message Christ brought with him, and constantly taught, was ONE message Only, The Kingdom of God Our Heavenly Father, and how WE are Son's; under the MOST HIGH. And that he came to Restore man back as a Son, and, in having Dominion once again, over this Earth; that Adam Lost. Christ came to RESTORE man's mindset (Repent - Change Your THINKING), back to KINGDOM mindset; and Sonship. This is the exact metaphor, and parable; of the Prodigal Son… For man is to be a Son to Our Heavenly Father, and have complete Dominion and domination, over this vast piece of Lovely Real Estate; called Earth.   And everything is to be yielded to Him/Us, from this position of authority. For Adam, from the very beginning was able to rule the world from this position of authority, by his WORDS ALONE, until he fell from dominion, and lost his position of authority; when he ate the forbidden fruit. Tsk, Tsk, Tsk…

Therefore, when Jesus spoke to the crowds, he informed them to make their words; work for them. For your WORDS have POWER. Christ advised "I've come to restore you. For Earth does not move by works, Earth is moved by words. This is part of your Dominion entitlement". And the crowds loved hearing this. For every time Jesus spoke to the masses, his truthful words; resonated within their Spirit. That was obviously the (Governor - the Holy Spirit) within them, assuring the people; who they are supposed to be.

Yet, when Christ would go into the synagogues and speak, many of the Pharisees and the High Priest of that religious Faith, rose up against him, continuously; contradicting everything he said. For they would say, "who is this man coming against us. Isn't he the son of Joseph (the carpenter); and Mary. He's never studied amongst us. Never a Disciples of our higher learning. How dare he come in, and teach this Kingdom mindset". And it was from then, that they started conspiring against him; for his life.

And Jesus did one thing, and one thing only; he preached the Kingdom of God.
Matthew 24:4 - 14
He taught nothing, other than - the Kingdom of God.
He never talked about himself.

FEDDOR

He never spoke about the cross, though he knew it was coming.

He never talked about what was to come with him.

He preached only the GOOD NEWS message of the Kingdom.

He said over and over in Parables, "the Kingdom of God is like….."

And again, "the Kingdom of God is like a man that….."

And so forth, and so on.

You (the reader), may go into your search engine and reference all the places in our Constitution (the Bible), that states where Jesus said: the Kingdom of God is like; and read for yourself - independently.

And for you Theologians, you can go straight to your Constitution and look it up yourself; with its glossary. Hit up all the reference points, and do your independent research; for validation.

Therefore, let it be understood; Jesus NEVER talked about himself. For he is a POLITICIAN, he spoke only about the Kingdom of God Our Heavenly Father; and this immensely infuriated the High Priest.

Case in point of their disdain towards him, occurred once when Christ was in the synagogue;

and he rose up to speak. It was on a Sabbath day.
And as he walked to the front of the audience,
passing all the High Priests and Pharisees, he
spotted (amongst this audience) a crippled woman
(who was always there on Sabbath day); whose
body was doubled over and bent. Christ looked
directly at her, and yearning zeal burned through
his eyes; towards her. Immediately, both the High
Priest and Pharisees observed his gaze upon her,
and they said within themselves "he's going to do
something. Doesn't he recognize it's the Sabbath
day". And Christ, perceiving their thoughts, looks
at them and says, "which of you, if you're mule fell
into a ditch on the Sabbath day; wouldn't go and
fetch him out. How much more should this
daughter not receive her healing, regardless of
what day it is. Is she not a child of God, and a
daughter of Abraham". And from thence, he
proceeded to tell the woman to straighten up her
back, and to be healed. And the woman did as he
instructed, and received her healing.
Ohhhh. For the High Priests, that was a No No..
They were enraged. For Christ had such a large
following, that the people freely went to him,
without hesitation, abandoning the religious
leaders; and the High Priests (who have been

Failing Them). And the High Priest and religious leaders conspired against Christ, advising, "this man is affecting our income; and economics. We must destroy him. Because the people follow after him, and they turn away from us. This is NOT ALLOWED".

Again, the main message Christ preached from the very very beginning was, "repent; for the kingdom of God has arrived".
Repent means to Change your Thinking…..
Repent Doesn't mean to be Sorrowful and Mournful, and to Cry out to God your sins; that's being REMORSEFUL…
God never said to be remorseful, that's just a natural emotional human reaction. Repent, Change your thinking; to the mindset of Our Heavenly Father. Christ said Repent, (change your thinking); for the Kingdom of God has arrived.

We give out annually Christmas Greetings cards, displaying this caption from The Book of Isaiah. It is also a Christmas song.
And Linus, from the "Charlie Brown Christmas Special" does a spotlighted solo performance addressing this fact; from Isaiah 9.

THE ULTIMATE POLITICIAN

"For unto us a child is born, unto us a son is given: and the Government shall be upon his shoulders, and his name shall be called Wonderful, Counselor, The Mighty God, The Everlasting Father, The Prince of Peace".

For Jesus when he first began preaching and ministering and talking to the people in the crowd, he said one thing, "Repent; for the Kingdom of God has arrived". For the original plan of God was to extend his Heavenly Kingdom, here on Earth, through; and for man. This is what is known as Colonization.

And to establish a family of Son's here on Earth, not servants. For religion, and a religious mindset; wants man to be servants. God doesn't want servants, God wants SON'S.

Proof of this fact & truth, is the story of The Prodigal Son.

Religion always makes man into servants, and long suffering. God doesn't want servants, he only wants Son's.

FEDDOR

In the story of the Prodigal Son, when he (the Son) returns home after squandering all of his father's fortune given to him; thinking to be a servant in his father's house. Instead, His father IMMEDIATELY gives him (his son) a Ring, a Robe, and Slippers, and says; "My Son was once lost and is now Found".

The father placed the ring on his son's finger, assuring his identity with the family. He then placed a robe of Nobility upon his back, signifying he's of Royalty; and his status as a Son of the King. And he placed slippers upon his feet, placing him back on right familial status and graces within their family's position - as a Son; with NO questions asked. And then the father killed the fattest calf, in celebration of the life of his Son's return home. That is LOVE. This is the Love Our Heavenly Father has for us. He is a Wonderful, and Merciful Father, that has wiped away ALL of our past rebellious acts (sins); with no questions asked. As long as we acknowledge him as Our Heavenly Father, and all that he did in restoring us back; to all that Adam lost.

And understand, Our Heavenly Father "God" is King. He is King of ALL Kings. And we (too) are also Kings, under him. This is the Kingdom concept. We are never servants, we are Son's; under the Most High.

For the Kingdom Gospel Message is called the Good News. And it is NOT a religion. For religion Oppresses man. Yet, the Good News Gospel message, of Our Heavenly Father - frees man.

For Jesus came to establish a Commonwealth of Citizens, NOT religious people; and NOTHING involved with (any) religious organization.

For a Son is a Legal citizen, under the King. All other individuals (non Sons) upon Earth, are illegal aliens. And Sons has Dominion on this Earth, (that he shall Possess Forever); as a legal heir to his entitled rights.

Our Heavenly Father calls us Sons of God, not Christians. The word Christians was given from the Romans, for it is truly a pagan term. We are never to be called by this Pagan title. We are Sons, and we are Believers of God, Our Heavenly Father; nothing (remotely) related to the standards of a pagan.

And as a son and a citizen of Our Heavenly Father's Kingdom, (here on earth); we receive All rights from our Government's Kingdom. And it is always granted happily from Our Heavenly Father, who would never withhold anything that is good; from us.

When Jesus came, nobody could place an accountability on him, because nobody knew who he was; except (in being) the son of Joseph and Mary. For he came into existence by way of a certain religious group (conduit), because of a covenant God made with Abraham. Yet, he came (ONLY) representing the Government; of Our Heavenly Father's Kingdom. For Christ came as a Dignitary and a Politician. And he came here teaching and preaching the Kingdom of God Doctrine and Message, to ALL people, about their inherit Citizenship; and Rights as a Son. And again (as said), the religious leaders and High Priests didn't like him and his message; and conspired against him. Whereas the throng and masses loved him, and his teachings. And they loved Christ teaching them on how (and to know), that they are sons; and not servants. And he advised them not to be religious people. Yet, the high religious leaders didn't like this, (for it was a personal attack on their livelihood), and they began conspiring physical harm against him; because the masses gravitated strongly to Christ. For Christ's message of the Kingdom resonated (Strongly) within their spirits (the masses), and immediately they knew it was all true; and that they were being Hoodwinked by the church/religious leaders.

And as a Kingdom Citizen, and Son; Our Heavenly Father pays off all of our debts. This only comes from Faith and understanding that he owns everything, and we as his son's ought to have no Secular cares; for we recognize we are heirs. For it is said and believed upon, that Our Heavenly Father takes very good care of his Son's needs; Always.

When Christ came, he came to establish a commonwealth of citizens. Commonwealth means, that everything owned by the King, is shared with his Citizen Son's; as rightful entitlement.

For the Bible (our Constitution) says, my God "Kingdom" shall supply all of my needs, according to his riches and Glory; by Christ Jesus. For God owns everything, and he is Our (Abba - Source) Father, and we are his citizen Son's, and he takes care of his own, us; and everything for us.

And in Our Kingdom, instead of the subjects dying for the King via war, Our Heavenly Father "God - The King" came to Earth in the flesh, and died for us; his son's.   Because only his blood was the most precious and pure (untouched and of no lineage), and was the only precious substance that could cover us, and to redeem us from the treasonous act that Adam did, when he gave up his position of Dominion - to the adversary, who was cast out of Heaven with no form; (dust) to the atmosphere.

For we all are the rightful property of Our Heavenly Father. And Our Heavenly Father is so merciful, allowing us time to realize this information of divine revelation, knowledge, via messages, literature as such (these writings), and people we come into contact with, in our daily walks, reminding us; that we are Property of God. We are Son's to Our Heavenly Father, which means - we are of Nobility. Royalty. The Ultimate Royalty of existence, from the King of Kings; Our Heavenly Father. Citizen

Son's we are, and we are afforded inherent entitled rights, when we come to the realization of who God is in our lives, and why we are here, and our Purpose in representing him, in this Colonized extension of the Kingdom of Heaven; here on Earth.

And this is extended to every single person, for those who are already; or become - Believers.

And God's plan is for a relationship with his sons, and never a religion. For NOTHING contained in a religion is represented in anything of God, Our Heavenly Father.   Man made religion. God ONLY wants a relationship with son's, not a religion.

Christ came here in the flesh, from God, and he brought with him a Government; of the Kingdom of Heaven. This Government (now here on earth), is to mirror Heaven; this is what Colonization is all about.

When you colonize a people you strip them of their past, (including their sins and sinful nature); and you give them a new identity. For Christ does not remember your past sins. And with this in mind, he wants you to keep moving forward; Not Looking

Back. Knowing has taken on all your sins, so long as you have repented (changed your past way of Thinking), and understand you're a son; that you belong to God. And that you're to live accordingly (per our Constitution), as a Son. That you may possess eternal life in Glory, here on this Paradise of Earth (our Dominion & Domain), that has been restored to us; for our Eternal Spirits.

This is what's interesting with the concept of Colonization. An example of this is Slavery/Enslavement.   For the Slave was stripped of his identity, and all of his connections with his past. Though Enslavement is a hard association of the Kingdom, Colonization is still under this same pretense. Strip them of their past (wipe away their sins), and never allow them to remember it (For God forgave ALL), and have them assume a new identity (New Creation) never to recollect on the past (it's all forgiven); and to keep moving forward (your Purpose).

Kingdom Colonization is a beautiful form of Colonization, in contrast to that of (man's) despotic, tyrannical enslavement; of his brother.

Let's ask now the big question:
Who is the most important person on Earth?

THE ULTIMATE POLITICIAN

Of course, the first person to come to mind is obviously - the Pope.
But the Pope is not the most important person on Earth. He is the most powerful person of the secular world, but he is not the most important.

Next, one might say the President of a country, particularly a powerful country; such as the United States of America.
But no, neither is this person the most important person on Earth.

Next, people might say a King or Queen of a strong Industrial Nation, or a Sultan over an oil Dynasty; and so forth.
Yet, neither are any of these the most important persons.

Nor are any of the Billionaires, and if exist any Trillionaires, for they too are not the most important person; whomever they might be.

The most important person on Earth is:

The Governor......

FEDDOR

The Governor

For the Governor is the HOLY SPIRIT, given to us from Our Heavenly Father.

And per our Constitution (the Bible), it advises that the Holy Spirit (the Governor); is in fact a PERSON.

God has arranged it that the Holy Spirit shall remain upon EVERY man on Earth, not a religion upon every man. And that he (man) has CONSTANT access to the Holy Spirit. For it is the Holy Spirit's Responsibility, to get the man to take on the mindset of his Heavenly Father; "Colonization". Man is to act like God. Talk like God, and operate in FULL Capacity; as that of Our Heavenly Father.

Man has been given Free Will, and God will never force himself upon you. For even God (himself) can't touch the Free Will of man. Man, would have to make a Conscious and Rational decision, to take on this MINDSET (Repent - Change Your Thinking), and understand he's a SON; to the Most HIGH.

It is a MINDSET that stems from your Faith and Ideology, that this is ALL REAL. For it is

FEDDOR

Impossible for man to figure out Spiritual things, with a secular mind. He must release all secularness (in thought), and comprehend this through the Spirit - in Faith.

And once man grasps this mindset (in Faith), knowing who he is (and who's He is), and functioning (talking and being) like Our Heavenly Father, and grasping our ENTITLED RIGHTS, via our Constitution (the Bible), thus causes the Holy Spirit (the Governor), connecting us directly to Our Heavenly Father, and HE (the Governor - Holy Spirit) will quicken in OUR Consciousness ALL Right Doings, and will Provoke us to Always do All things Proper; and Orderly....

For Our Heavenly Father is all about ORDER...

And be it understood, the Holy Spirit (Governor) cannot make you learn.

Osmosis (in learning) is not real.

Man must pick up his Constitution (the Bible), read; and learn.

And he must engulf himself around other Sons of God, to learn his proper place as a son; here upon this Earth.

Man has complete Free Will given him from God, from the very beginning of creation. God gave him free will to do as he pleases. For God is orderly.

God told (Adam) from the very beginning, giving him complete instructions; of what he Can and Cannot DO.

Man has a free will to choose, and God (will) never interfere with it; and neither will the adversary. All that the adversary can do is put thoughts into (man's) imagination, enticing him (tempting); to act upon a conceived thought. For the adversary's ONLY ambition is to cause man to speak death and destruction to his own life, and talk one's self out of his Own Rightful Inheritance. Yet, in retrospect, God has given man the Holy Spirit (the Governor), advising man CONSTANTLY; "don't be fooled by the adversary. You have authority over him. Stay focussed and intact with all you possess, that is rightfully YOURS, via entitlement as a Son; to The Most High. For he the adversary, LOST EVERYTHING, especially; his BEAUTY. And he's Hatefully MAD".

Before Christ arrived here in the flesh upon Earth, the Holy Spirit (the Governor) only came sporadically. And after Christ came, prior to ascending back to the Kingdom, he left the Holy Spirit (the Governor) to remain behind forever; for each and every man upon Earth.

FEDDOR

Yet, prior to Christ's arrival on earth, the Holy Spirit sporadically took form, appearing himself from within; and through man. An example of this was through Samson, pulling down the columns - killing tens of thousands of Philistines, after they had plucked his eyes out and shaved his head bald; Rendering him strengthless

Another example, Noah when it came time to build the Ark, that housed all the animal species, and Man, that still survives today; were upon that Ark. For ONLY the Holy Spirit (the Governor) could have performed this task, through Noah. For Noah was a singular man, along with his sons that assisted; to accomplish this impossible task. For when God gives you an assignment, it will always be the impossible, that you may not receive the credit, yet - glorifying God, who gets All the credit, and you were the instrument vessel (The Holy Spirit worked through); receive all the benefits and the rewards. God set it up this way. Noah and his family were the only survivors. And Life After the flood, and everything upon the Earth, are direct descendants from that lineage; for there was no other life upon Earth.

And there are other times throughout the Bible (The Old Testament) when the Holy Spirit showed up, performed its miracle; and left….

Another example, with Abraham. When he was about to slay Isaac (his son), the Lord stopped him, (via an Angel), when he saw the great love Abraham had for him; (Our Heavenly Father). And the Angel prevented him from slaying Issac, and set up a lamb caught in the thicket (briar) to be used (instead of Issac); as the sacrifice.

There are more and more instances where the Holy Spirit shows up, performed; and left. All prior to Christ's arrival.
Do your research.

And now, the Holy Spirit is permanently upon Earth, and available for each and every man that chooses to live a life accepting the Lord Sovereign (Adonai), as Our Heavenly Father, and we as Son's; by this the Holy Spirit is assigned to us… This is All A FREE GIFT from Our Father…..

It is important that you are indoctrinated with this correct dialogue of necessary information. I am very well aware that I am repeating myself numerous times, over and over again; with much of the same information. It is important that I do this, to indoctrinate you, that it's grasped into your memory; and consciousness. That your spirit grasps it, and understands that these are your entitled rights.   And I will do so throughout this composition in other areas discussed, to its end. That you may understand ALL of your entitled rights, via our Constitution; the Holy Bible.

For the adversary, none other than Satan (himself), who was cast out of Heaven and has NO physical form, tries to steal this information from you and ROB you of your identity, and all of your entitled rights from our Constitution - the Holy Bible, and all of God's written words that says; you as a (SON) are entitled to….

One must read this information, Over, and over, and over again,   indoctrinating your mind with these Truths, and increase your readings independently, attending seminars that are teaching the kingdom of God message, concept, ideology, and way of Thinking/Knowing Sonship - of man here on Earth, in the form of God (Character), Thinking and Acting like God (for HE Loves this), yet understanding he (man); is underneath the Most High. For we are Son's, never servants…

For in all of the trio of God, (Father, Son, and Holy Spirit), the most misunderstood entity is the most important person here on Earth, and this is the Holy Spirit; The Governor.

Misunderstood is an understatement.

Oftentimes, you see religious people thinking they are affected by the Holy Spirit, (the Governor), but in fact they're just acting out; on (self) Emotions. Some of these (religious) people will be in church, jumping around, convulsing, and think that that's the Holy Ghost; it's NOT.

Others will do various things, feats, and fits; for ATTENTION. Acting out and claiming that it's the Holy Spirit.   IT'S NOT….

The Holy Spirit is ORDERLY, and never seeks ATTENTION.   Everything with God, Our Heavenly Father, is orderly.

Therefore, if you see anyone acting out (religious people), and it doesn't seem to be orderly, or doesn't click with your Spirit; chances are it's definitely NOT the Holy Spirit. Yet and still, religious people (and they are numerous), will try to claim it as from God; Our Heavenly Father. Our (ABBA) Father is orderly, in Everything.

FEDDOR

Religion

Religion is completely Man-Made.

God never set up religion. God said to be a believer in him, for God loves ALL people; not ONE particular religion.
Yes, Christ came into existence (via the conduit); by way of the Seed of Abraham.
Yet, God never said that was the chosen religion.
God said that they shall be Priests and teachers to the world, (IF & so long) as they keep his Commandments.

I like something that the late great Paul Mooney (comedian) said on religion. He said "when man cannot take these Ten Commandments that God instructed us to live by, (Precepts), that man says; this is too much. This is truly a bit too much for us to live by. Let's go and create a religion to live by, and a new way of worship; and make new (amended) Commandments. For these original Ten Commandments, put too much of God's foot; in man's ASS".

FEDDOR

Hhhmmmmmmm…

Of course I paraphrased, but you get the gist.

And it's true….

Society for some reason (now) is governed by this way of thinking, and living. By this Free Will (and God gave us free will); and free lived lifestyle. For in society (within the past recent decades), when God's original Ten Commandments became too hard and pressing for man to live by, that he (now) chooses to do his own thing, yet, under the pretense of a religion; that is presumed to be connected to Heaven. Well, this is completely Unacceptable. For God set precepts (Rule & Laws), for a reason; and we are to live by them - NO QUESTIONS ASKED…..

For he is the King, the Most High, Our Creator; he makes the Laws…..

Now, let us reflect. A kingdom is a Country, not a religion. We (Son's) are to be the reflection of God's Colony. His Kingdom in Heaven, here on Earth. Let me say that again.

We are to be a Colony reflecting the Kingdom of God's Heaven, HERE on Earth. Earth is a Colonized colony of the Kingdom.

Religion does an outstanding job at keeping man away from God. That's why the adversary is NOT threatened by religion. He actually Embraces it. For it is part of his Manifesto, that man has a sense of religion; forgetting about the Good News of the Kingdom & His PURPOSE. And it's been working.
He is Brilliant.

God created us to have dominion over Earth, not Heaven. And not for us to go to Heaven, yet, to be here forever - Heaven on Earth.
Heaven is only for God.

God created us in His image, which means - in his personality, his nature, his character; that's his image. This is everything that Jesus (The Ultimate Politician) preached when he was here on Earth. For he never talked about himself, nor to worship Him.

Your personality is considered the Glory of God. For this is the reflection of the Holy Spirit, (the Governor) Within.

And be mindful, that God never allowed anything to grow on Earth, (from the beginning), because there was no one (MAN); to manage it. God then sent man. For man is to manage this piece of Real Estate. And for man, who's in God's image, is to have Dominion over this entire Earth, this massive Beautiful Land; of Lush - Real Estate.

Christ always taught the crowds how God brought Heaven to Earth. That was his purpose for man, to colonize and dominate this land, as well as to act and think as God; here on Earth. For Christ knew ahead of time that (via - under the guise of religion), the adversary was going to start attacking this gender (male) - throughout Society; Worldwide.

The Male is important to God, because the male is the foundation of God's human family, for the male is full of seeds; God's seeds.

Jesus, while teaching, often spoke about how the male is important to God, because we (male's) are God's strategy here on Earth, and the devil knows this; and he's afraid of us males.

Keep in mind the male (Dad), in the home is Destiny.

So if the man goes away, so also goes the Nation.

Therefore, don't push the male (man) out.

This caption causes me to ponder on the movie "The Color Purple" when character Shug Avery was wailing, while in the tub - in a drunken state - advises "I never know a girl to turn out right; when she has no father around to guide her".

So True.

Jesus also talked about and proclaimed, that most problems in society (oftentimes) is the lack of the male (the father); in the home.

If you want to know what society looks like, look at the family. For the family is the Prototype of what's going on in society.

Focus on the family and you automatically strengthen Society.

And if you want a better Government, and the prevention of National immorality; you have to have a better family structure.

Again, The male is very important to God, for he first established his Covenant - with the first male; Adam.

And because the adversary knows that the male is so important to God, therefore, what - does he do, he always goes after the woman; for he is not afraid of them. Case and point, he first grabbed Eve.

And unfortunately, many men have been chased out of their home's by the tongues of a woman (Jezebel spirited) in today's society, thus causing the children (especially Son's); being reared by the female. Not that the son is feminized, but he is often indoctrinated by her views.

One of the main things a man needs, in and throughout his entire life, is to increase in Knowledge (light). For even the Bible - our Constitution says, "my people perish for a lack of knowledge". BOOKS… Read and Learn.

If you're going to be a leader, you must continuously read and study in order to Be an Effective man, and a pillar in society; let alone your household. Be it understood, when a woman sees a man with a vision, and knows that he's going places, she will stick with him, through thick and thin; like the R&B song "wherever you go - I will follow".

And understand something very important, if you were born a male you're a male; but you're not a man. A man comes from development. Time must be invested in him, that he learns what it takes to be a man; and being taught how to be a man. For this is a learning process, as in almost Everything in Life - is a learned behavior; all in a Learning Process.

Being born a male is a natural biological reality. Being a MAN is a Spiritual process. To be a man comes with much development, training; and learned behavior.

Per Genesis, it says: God made two species of human, male and female; and God established the Covenant with the male.

And in Genesis, (our Constitution), God says: all that he created was Very Good. Therefore, there are NO mistakes in anything; nor Anyone. For ALL that God made is very good, and Perfect.

FEDDOR

And as a result of this, man in his vast research in understanding the human anatomy - and trying to play God without the Power of the Lord, has interfered in many things, biological and genetics - (Eugenics), and has attacked the human chromosomes; provoking the human body to not be in the PERFECT form as God started with. Hmmmm..

Therefore, when a man is not acting like himself, he is out of Character - of who he is to be; and who GOD made him to be.

And it has come to light that the number one need of a man is God.
Whereas the physical need of a man's human body is sex, and of course food, clothing; and shelter.

And the biggest difference between a man and a woman per creation, is that man is a logical creature, and a woman is emotional. This has been proven by science. For God established his Covenant with man, yet the adversary went after Eve; playing & preying off of her emotions.

Man must recognize that it is through his masculinity, there is found his purpose of life. And our purpose of life (Man) is to fulfill Our Father in Heaven's Mission, here upon the Earth, to dominate it and have Dominion, on this colonized planet; from the Kingdom.

Your value comes from your purpose, and knowing your purpose.

Therefore, if you remove a man out of a family, the family loses its purpose.
Keep in mind, your purpose is Always connected to your relationship, that goes for both in the natural; and the Spiritual,

It is so important that the male finds and knows his purpose, and be in constant communication; with his Heavenly Father.

The man must always think on the terms of his purpose, not the role of his identity. His identity (as a SON) comes from his connection to his/Our Heavenly Father, who guides him and informs him of his purpose, via (the Governor); the Holy Spirit.

FEDDOR

Our Constitution

"The Holy Bible"

Every Country, every Locale, every Province & also Kingdom, has either a Constitution, or some form of Parliamentary document; Governing its people.

It is important to read your Constitution, because it consists of your RIGHTS, of what you can and cannot do, and oftentimes they'll put in it consequences if these Rights, Laws, Rules & Precepts; are violated.

The Constitution is your Bundle of Legal Rights, of total Entitlement.

For the believer, our Constitution is our Holy Bible; God's written word.

This book, our Constitution, the "Holy Bible", is our bundle of legal rights, that the adversary does not

want you to know; what you are fully entitled to.
And if it wasn't for King James of England, who
sanctioned and got the Holy Bible translated along
with Tyndale, and having the Bible made public for
all Citizens; we would not know what we are
entitled to.
Read independently The Brilliance, by the same
author for further details on this.

Our Constitution, the Holy Bible - instructions of
things that you can do & cannot do, along with
consequences; and also what we are entitled to.
And one of the first things it discusses, is
everything that Adam did in his Treasonous Act -
when he lost Dominion over Earth; along with his
words NO LONGER carrying him.
And the same Constitution elucidates how Christ
came in the flesh, and restored man back to
everything; that Adam lost. And informs man how
he has total power and authority over the
adversary. And that God has every man that is a
believer as a Son, and as a son he has nothing to
worry about; because his yoke is easy to carry.
For Christ brought with him when he came (Isaiah
9), a Government upon his shoulders, making
God's Heavenly Kingdom an easy yoke; for man to
bear. Because God carries everything - himself.

THE ULTIMATE POLITICIAN

He wants man to think like him, and yield all credit and honor back to the Creator. Because he made all of this. Therefore, he made man to have control (Stewardship); over all of this. And to do so, God came down in the flesh, and restored man back to his rightful position. And he wants man to know who he is (a Son), and his purpose in having dominion over this real estate, and to walk and talk and act like God here on Earth; for this makes our Heavenly Father extremely proud.

Therefore, pick up your Constitution, your Holy Bible (read & learn) and know who you are, and all of your Bundle of Legal Entitled Rights; that cannot be stripped away from you.   This is how God ordained it, and set it up from the very beginning; of creation. Again, Adam and his treasonous act; in messing up. Yet, God had Redemption already set in motion, and brought us back into his will, all under the Covenant by HIS own Precious BLOOD; Covering Us. Setting us back in our rightful place and Position, as Sons; to the Most High.
The adversary hates this (truth & fact), because he lost all of this, when he fell from Heaven like lightning; as Jesus advised. He (the adversary), fell and lost everything; all because of conceit. For

FEDDOR

he was once the most beautiful angel in Heaven, heading the music and entertainment arena; in the entire Kingdom. And when he was CAST OUT and fell from Heaven (due to conceit), he neither (any longer) had beauty, nor form, yet turned into a pile of Ashes that had been thrown (fallen); into the atmosphere. And there he STILL remains.

So you are a King

In our Constitution, the Holy Bible - it says (and I paraphrase),
I am a little God, below GOD, the only thing higher than me is the Most High, in being God Our Heavenly Father (ABBA); Himself.
And Christ instructed us, when he spoke to the masses, as to how we are to pray, we are to say "Our Father Who Art in Heaven, &c"….
And this particular prayer gives complete reverence and recognition to Our Heavenly Father (in Heaven - his Domain), and that Earth (our permanent Domain); is to mirror Heaven.

When Christ came down here in the form of flesh of a man, (God on Earth), he was Limited to one (Human existence) body. Hence, he was not able to be God Our Heavenly Father (in Heaven for 33 1/2 years), everywhere & anywhere - all at one time; omnipotent. Instead, he was severely limited; For he was in one flesh. In doing so, taking on the form of a human (man), which humanistically limited him, yet - he still possessed all of his Godly Supernatural-ness, his Spirit, his

Drive, his Healing abilities; and all of his Goodness.

Well, when it was time for him to end his Earthly Mission, and now go through all leading up to the Cross, now comes onto the scene - Pontius Pilate. All the Jewish High Priests, Scribes, and Pharisees, had now conspired against Jesus, to Pontius Pilate (the Governor of that region); for his death. For they advised "this man (Jesus) who has never sat under our teaching, knows too much. And is leading away the crowds, our crowds. He is affecting our income and livelihood. And we don't like him, because he speaks blasphemously; calling himself the Son of God. Therefore, we wish to have him removed permanently; even unto death".   Needless to say, they arranged with Pilate; that he was to be executed.

Pontius Pilate soon thereafter met with Jesus, (after he was arrested), yet, Pilate advised later to those Priests; "I found NO Fault in him".

All because at the same time, Pilate's wife pulls Pilate to the side - and says, "hey, wait a minute. You know who this is? Right".

Pontius Pilate advises, "he's the guy that's going around saying he's the son of God. And the Jews Priests don't like it".

And the wife relents. "You better leave him alone. You know, he might NOT be lying. Because, I personally saw Him in action. And recently, I had a bad dream about all of this. A premonition of sorts, that something bad is going to happen; if you mess with him. I'm telling you, this guy is serious; and I think He's Real. I've seen him perform many of those healings, raising people from the dead, and restoring sight, and making the lame walk; and bent backs - straightened. I saw this. And now he's before your Courts. And you think you're going to say something against him (listening to those Priests). Hmmmm. You better watch yourself, and think twice. This man is NOT a regular man". And Pilate IMMEDIATELY took haste, to these words. For his wife's words pierced him. Yet, he still must perform the protocol of the Courts; towards the accused.

Therefore, Jesus was scourged, and then he was before Pilate; Face to Face.

Pilate says, "I'm looking at you. And the people say that you are a king. So are you a King"?

And Jesus didn't answer, only looked at him; (Pilate).

Then Pilate (feeling full of his authority) says, "you know what Authority I have over you. And what can be done"?

And in this INSTANCE, Jesus looked at him hard & piercingly; and snapped. And was ready to flesh out ALL OVER him, on this comment.   Because, case and point, (God - Jesus in the flesh) Created Pilate. Instead, Jesus remained reserved; and wasn't going to go there.

For I know Jesus was ready to snap and say, "what the "F" did you just now say. You, have authority over me? NEVER!! You Fool".

Instead, Jesus looked at him, and he said, "you have no authority over me, unless it was given to you from above; and that did not happen". And Jesus continued.   "Now do you know what Authority I have? I can call down ten (10) Legions of Angels. They're right there in the atmosphere, standing by; waiting - to take all this out. Waiting for my Command".

Pontius Pilate looked up and got scared. He immediately recollects upon the words his wife said to him, and now hears this subtle threat; directly from Jesus Christ lips. And again Pilate says, "So you are a King".

He continues, "I will have nothing to do with this. I wash my hands of this. It has nothing to do with me, let somebody else handle this". And he sent him back to the Jews. And Pilate advised the Priests, "I'm not having anything to do with this one".

For Pilate got scared, and rightfully so.

For Jesus' words quickened, and punched Pilate's inner spirit. For when Pontius Pilate looked up, into the atmosphere, I'm sure for a brief second those angels showed themselves to him.

Everyone of those ten (10) Legions of Angels, and then disappeared. Because they were ever present, yet; unseen. Jesus saw them all the time. Pontius Pilate literally got scared, and washed his hands of the case.

For the power of one's words from our mouth's, per our Constitution the Bible, says "that by our words we shall be acquitted; and by our words shall one be condemned". Therefore, choose your words wisely; over your own life.

Again, Pilate got scared when Jesus snapped; and looked at him. Thinking foolishly, that he had authority over Jesus. Well, Jesus instantly corrected him, without fleshing out on him; and allow the Angels to attack him & Earth. And Jesus advised Pilate, "you do not take my life, I Lay My Life down; freely. Therefore, let me correct you right now on the spot". And Pilate trembled at these words, for he knew immediately; Jesus truly was a KING.....

THE ULTIMATE POLITICIAN

Principalities and Angels

Both of these entities, creatures (if I may); are Real.

Principalities are recognizable, and often - so blatant, that one can see their visible manifestation; in certain communities.

Angels too are real, and you (too) can see them, but usually attached to a person. Though both of these creatures/entities are unseen by the naked eye, yet when you put on your spiritual eyes you can see them; by looking up into the atmosphere. For they often make themselves visible to the person looking, for a brief moment. As said in the word, our Constitution; "seek and ye shall find". They are present and always amongst us. For it is a known fact, there's a lot more going on above your head; than below your feet.

Both Principalities and Angels are genderless creatures (beings), created by Our Heavenly Father.

The Angels have been given charge to tend to us (Son's), Believers of Our Heavenly Father. And they are assigned to cater to us - when we pray to Our Heavenly Father, and he sets things (loose) in motion (when we pray), because man has Dominion on this Earth; his words carry him. For God sends the Angels to serve us, when we ask of him anything.

Be ye mindful, God is NOT coming down here because you prayed and asked him to fix your marriage, or to heal your body, or to fix your finances; and or any other perilous thing. He has done Everything already. He concluded ALL that he was going to do, by going to the Cross; shedding his Precious Blood. And has placed man in Authority, (Son's that is), here on Earth where we have dominion (once again - No thanks to Adam - messing up); and are to Dominate. He's done everything Already. Therefore, he advised the Angels to cater to us, and to grant us everything; that we request. For a Son thinks and acts like his Father "God", and will make reasonable and logical requests.

Whereas Principalities, these are also spirits that once lived in Heaven, that got cast out with the adversary; Lucifer.

FEDDOR

The interesting thing about History, it's not boring.
And the Bible, our Constitution is a History book of
chronological events, besides being a book that
lists all things (we) as Son's; are entitled to.
Well, the adversary lost his beautiful form and
position, in the utmost inner court - alongside Our
Heavenly Father, and got cast out via Michael the
Archangel, along with his minion (followers - once
angels now demon spirits); principalities. These
principalities (spirits), were cast out into the
atmosphere; and they are there wreaking havoc.
Havoc, because they're angry at all that they lost,
for they once were in paradise, and Now - cast into
the atmosphere; and eventually into the Lake of
Fire. So their purpose is to cause Havoc amongst
man, and his soul. For both God and the
adversary, are after man's soul.

For man is a spirit that has a soul, which lives in a
body.
And both God and the adversary (not enemy,
because an enemy has equal status with his
competitor, and the adversary DOES NOT, for he
is a created creature - by Our Heavenly Father),
are after man's soul; for OUR spirit lives forever.

Proof of Angels guarding over people, an example - a horrible motor vehicle accident, and people walking away from it; sometimes unscathed.

And principalities (proofs) in certain areas, you'll see certain lifestyles.

These lifestyles could be of a lascivious nature, in neighborhoods/communities, deviants, poverty and degradation in certain communities; and so forth.   All one has to do is look at the community, and see what is the lifestyle, that would give you an example; of what type of principality is manifested there. For principalities demons are spirits assigned to a particular area. And even to certain households. And you can see indications of this, at what type of things are taking place; within that structure. Depending on the unruliness or disorder, that's something is not quite correct.

And speaking on principalities, many times you see people that have certain predispositions; such as: gambling, or alcoholism; or what have you. Let's even say people possessing certain sexual proclivities. It is not their predisposition, and they are not born with this genetic (as many scientists try to say). You must equate it directly to the principality (demon spirit), that is plaguing that lineage, that has been assigned either to that area, or to that family; or that community. It is truly an evil spirit. It is not a predisposition, or a genetic flaw; for God makes Perfection. Remember in Genesis, God saw everything that he had made was good. Now man on the other hand (Scientist/Doctors - not all), gets in and starts tinkering genetically with what God has purposed, causing havoc; again principalities.

The way to break a stronghold of a principality is through your knowledge and awareness of that principality, and Knowing your Constitution (your Bible) of all your entitled rights; and Prayer & Faith.

Breaking that stronghold, for it is truly a stronghold, but it does not have to attach to you or your family (any longer); you have authority over it. God gave that back to us (Dominion & Domination), by going to the cross. Placing us back in dominion over this Earth, and we as Sons, to those of us; who believe in Him.

It is said you are known by The Company You Keep. Certain people attract certain things, therefore, you get what you attract; all too often.

If a person keeps getting the same thing over and over again in a relationship, or in friendships; that's the type of persona they are exhuming. If they want change, they must do what is known; (repent - change your thinking). Change your conversation, and your communication, and your lifestyle will automatically change; along with the people in your environment.

As said, "you are what you eat", whatever you're taking in, both visually & mentally; that's who you become.

Angels are real (creature) beings.   Remember, Angels are genderless. Therefore, they are not up in Heaven preying upon people, swooping down; and having sex with them. Nor are the demon spirits, even though they were kicked out of heaven. They too are genderless. So that myth of somebody having a demon's baby, or baby of the devil, or something about (giant people) being children of Angels; are all Myths. Angels and spirits are genderless. They do not procreate. Procreation was only set up for man, for he is to populate the world with Our Heavenly Father's Colony; here on Earth. That's how God instructed him, for man is a bundle of seeds (within his testicles), and woman is an incubator, incubating the man's seed, which is part of the Covenant mission between Man & God; Our Heavenly Father.

Angels are ever present, they are everywhere. See the Unseen. Look with your spiritual eyes. Look into the atmosphere and your surroundings, you will see them. When you go into the spirit Realm, they are ever present, always around us, always ready to assist; upon our demand/command.

You must call upon God, and make your request known, and he sets loose his angels; to assist us. For Our Heavenly Father is in Heaven, yet - he gave Dominion to man, here on Earth. And he (demands) us to think and act like him. Not run to him like a crying baby, every time you stub your toe. He wants you to have Authority, and know our position; as Sons.   We are to know who we are. To know what Jesus restored us back to, through his Redemptive blood. To know we are son's. That we are little Gods here on Earth, underneath the Most High. That we think and act like him. And then we say to Our Heavenly Father, loose those Angels, and bring forth whatever I need; for I'm on Kingdom Purpose. It could be finances, food & raiment, peace & Harmony, needed vacation & relaxation, &c, whatever you asked for; God sits loose. We have at our disposal both Michael the (Warrior) Archangel, and Gabriel (the messenger). And they both will send forth all necessary Angels, needed to come; to our Aid. The first thing we need to do is, set your WORDS in Motion.

God gave us back our authority of our WORDS having Full Effect and Influence, in our lives. And (US) knowing our position of authority, as a Son; and Sonship. He loves this. He says, "Look at my boy. Talking and acting like me! That's what I like". For Kingdom Colonization is about getting man to think and act like God, and having his words do everything for HIM.

God knows everything you want and need, you need not ask for it. Yet, because we live in this world system, you are to talk and get your words flowing, speaking positive words over your life, and that of your families; and friends. And when they are set in motion, they come to pass.

The adversary hates this, because this is what he lost.

FEDDOR

He got cast out of Heaven, and his minions; and none of them have any Authority any longer. They have no form, and they were cast into the atmosphere. All they can do is try to play (attack) in the realm of your imaginations and thoughts. Remember, repent means to change your thinking. Jesus "The Ultimate Politician" came here to retrain man to think like God. That he is God on Earth, under the Most High.

Again, God ALWAYS wants us Thinking and Acting - like him.

It is understood that we live in this current world system, and that there are (other) outside influences, ie., politicians, the media, social media; and so forth. And all too often these mentioned groups possess ideologies that DO NOT resonate with many people, (Sons) who possess a Kingdom's mindset.

It is most important when one is voting in Politicians, person's of Governmental high positions, Chief Justices, Congress, and &c., that one understands their ideology, their belief system; and how they feel about certain things. This is extremely important because this affects you, your children, your schools, your community; and &c. This now ties back into principalities.

If these certain politicians do not line up with your standards in ideology, and your belief system, and they are proclaiming other things that's contrary to what you believe, then you (the Son & citizen) are to become a sounding voice; making things known of your disapproval. For this COMPLETELY falls under the realm of the Kingdom mandate.

We are to always remember that our Earth reflects Our Heavenly Kingdom. Many areas do not reflect this, therefore change must take place. Again (repent) change your thinking.   Change your mindset, and your life/lifestyle, and your community; will change.

Start with your life, then your household, it will eventually span out into your community; and continue to spread. This (truth) is so important.

I could say much in this area, and in various other areas of (hot topic) discussions, yet, this is something to be done independently by the reader, researching on principalities and community effects/affects.   For I can not spoon-feed everything to you. One must be given a seed of information, and then the reader must take initiative and research independently the things they are eager to have information upon. I will say

though, dealing with principalities - is a Very
Serious Matter.

It's unfortunate, many churches, even "the
Christian Churches", (though this is a pagan title -
christian); are NOT preaching this Kingdom of God
message. For I can say much on the Kingdom of
God, and information, yet, again - I only lay a
seed; it is up to the reader to independently
research this message for further enhancement.
The Kingdom of God is for everyone - Worldwide.
For God loves people. God loves ALL people.
He is Our Heavenly Father, and he set up his
"Colonized" Kingdom here on earth; for every
single person. And he left the Holy Spirit - the
Governor, in our lives.

The Kingdom of God was NOT designed for any
one particular group (only), or a certain religion;
Never - Ever - Ever....

God our Heavenly Father loves everyone.
Even the biggest sinner, or even the biggest
atheist; God loves that person. He's the creator of
that person too.   They are (hurting & searching).
For something has happened, in their lives to
make them turn away from God, to question his
love; or his Deity. Maybe someone has harmed
them, (including religious groups, which is Man

made), giving them misinformation; or treated them poorly.

God wants them to seek him out personally. And he will have his ministering Angels go to them, and seek them out - and bring them the right person, message, or even this particular composition - into their lives; to help them comprehend his love.

For the Bible (our Constitution) says, "seek and ye shall find".

This is the ONLY message Jesus spoke of, the Kingdom of God.

He Always advised, the Kingdom has Everything. Nothing is lacking in the Kingdom.

The Kingdom provides (for his Sons) everything. All the benefits, and all the entitlement of a (citizen/son), here on Earth are provided for you; from the Kingdom.

Unfortunately, the religious groups have hidden this information, or they don't even know this; for themselves.

And as we are aware, those High Priests listening to him (Christ/Yeshua) acknowledged this information to the crowds, got jealous; and they wanted his head.

The Garden

Eden means in the presence of God

I'm certain that when Christ (The Ultimate Politician) was in the synagogue speaking, or before the crowds in public, that the High Priests, the Chief Magistrates, and other Officials over the crowds; marveled at the things mentioned. For Christ NEVER sat under their tutelage. For he spoke in First Person Singular. This astounded and aggravated these high-minded religious people, and groups. Because he spoke as if he was God himself. And Jesus reading their thoughts knew that they perceived him as a blasphemer. He didn't let that bother him. For he continued in his delivery and the people (crowds) loved it. The High Priests saw him as a heretic and lunatic.

For Jesus probably said things in the nature - as such:

"Thank you for the allowance of me being before you. Let's go back briefly, to the very beginning with ABBA (Father - God), Adam and Eve; in the garden. When Adam fell from Dominion, after eating; the forbidden fruit".

Be it understood, much more information on this topic can be acquired in reading this selfsame author's "Posterity".

Christ continues. "The adversary has no form, for he fell from Heaven like lightning. Mere dust into the atmosphere. I know, for I observed All. The adversary is a cunning creature. His art is his best skill, and it's with his tongue. You see, he headed my musical arena in the Kingdom. Well, though he was cast out, ABBA-Father does not reclaim any gifts disseminated. And the adversary possessed a great talent in the art of words, music; & entertainment. He was exceptional in his talent. And did I fail to mention his beauty. Well, this too was his pinnacle. The most beautiful Angel (creature) ever created. Now, he's dust. Therefore, he observed ABBA - Father, and the creation of ALL Things; including Man. And now he sees ABBA - Father, discussing with Adam (man), All things, and forges a covenant with Adam. And he overheard from a distance, when

FEDDOR

ABBA - Father told Adam, NEVER to touch the tree in the midst of the garden; of Knowledge - Good & Evil. So, the adversary, after hearing this, knew he had to somehow get into Eden (the Presence of God); there in the garden. So the adversary smoothly convinced the serpent, in the allowance of entering his physical body, because dust has NO Physical FORM, yet; it could speak. Remember, his GREATEST talent are his WORDS.... So the serpent was wooed over, and allowed the adversary to enter into him".

To the readers, from this point on as Christ speaks (in this portion of the composition) when we mention the serpent in the garden, it is actually the adversary we are talking about. For the serpent is now possessed by the adversary, and is in a state of comatose; while the adversary utilizes his body.

Christ continues. "So the serpent knew he had to get inside that inner area, where both Abba Father and Adam; were in Council. So, being the cunning and conniving creature that he is, decides his best plan of attack; was EVE. And the serpent smoothly and stealthily slithered over to Eve, and began ingratiating her with much flattery, acting like he knew nothing of the conversation; between

Abba - Father and Adam. And the serpent told
Eve, how nice of a body - God made of her. And
how it is incredible, that he took part of Adam, and
made this voluptuous woman. And that she looks
nothing like Adam. Yet, she came out of him. He
complimented her beautiful looks. Her fair
flawless porcelain skin. Her thick luscious silky
hair. Her curvy hips, flat stomach, small waist, her
supple breast; and her beautiful private parts. All
for Adam's pleasure & delight. Eve blushed and
acted shy, from all of the weighted Flattery. She
loved it and took it all in, which rendered her weak
and defenseless; for his incoming attack. Vanity,
he knows this sin and weakness - all too well. And
his plan worked.

So he beguiled the woman, because he knew she
was weak. For he knew that the Covenant was
with Adam, so he had to use Eve; for his master
plan of attack. Prior to doing all of this and
confronting Adam, he first discussed with Eve
everything about the tree of Knowledge - of Good
and Evil. And he went over details with her,
though she tried to negate him, but he kept
flattering her, and she kept laughing and giggling;
and enjoying the compliments. And then he said,
present the fruit to your mate - Adam. And have

him eat it. And if he refuses to eat of the fruit, caress your voluptuous body, and let him see all the goodies you have, and let him know what good things you will do to him; after he eats the fruit. Get him to be weak, like soft clay beneath your toes; from the river side.   He'll then do whatever you ask. Show him those pretty curvy hips, and wiggle & jiggle in front of him; your supple breast. He'll do whatever you ask. He's a MAN. Eve laughed and giggled, blushed with tender shyness; and went along with the plan".

Christ continues. "Eve now bestowes to Adam, all information bestowed to her; from the serpent. For the serpent had convinced Eve that if she partook of the fruit, that both she and Adam would be just like God; equal to Him. But she was foolish, because they were already like God. For the conniving serpent convinced her to doubt herself. For self-doubt is one of his greatest tricks. The serpent was so slick that he persuaded her to taste the fruit, and advised - nothing would happen. And being the inquisitive and emotionally pulled person that she (Eve) was, she listened and tried; and nothing happened.   And Eve exclaimed - it just tasted like fruit. Well, now Eve did everything that the serpent told her to do, with her body, to seduce Adam; in order for him to eat of the fruit. Though Adam at first refused, she continued salaciously pursuing him - by jiggling and gyrating in front of him, moseying around, sashaying and provocatively walking before him; all in The Art of Seduction. For Eve freely took on completely, the spirit of a Jezebel. Adam now was completely aroused (wink-wink), and ready for (some horizontal) action. When she smoothly presented him the fruit to be consumed, prior to any action getting started between them; at that (very) moment. For he was spoiled, well accustomed to being inside of her ever since she was formed - from him; and placed as his helpmate. For he lived within her bosom. And being weak and vulnerable, due to his hormones getting the best of him, he (impulsively) bit the fruit, all for the sake of momentous pleasure; with Eve".

Christ continues. "Well now the snare was set and caught. For the Covenant was set up with Adam. EVERYTHING changed when Adam bit the fruit. ABBA Father-God gave all instructions to Adam, I know he (Adam) in turn relinquished the same instructional information over to Eve - in private, that they are NOT to touch the tree; of knowledge - of Good and Evil. And it is understood, and believed - that forbidden tree in the midst of the garden, was never submerged in the ground. That this tree was actually elevated, buoyant - above the surface of the Earth, standing out and understood; DON'T TOUCH…. Well, being the inquisitive persons they both were, listened to the serpent who had beguiled them; and advised innocently - ooh let's taste".

Christ continued. "And Unfortunately, destruction came Immediately; for ALL Man. Which brings ME (Yeshua) into this event, and here I am (now) before you"…

Christ continues. "The serpent did not lie, he slandered the truth. Slander is to tell the truth of something, resulting in Devastating Consequences. For slander is speaking the truth, that will cause hurtful, damaging; and harmful effects.   And this one was catastrophically harmful.   Treason at that".

Christ continues. "Anyhow, immediately ABBA-Father was there, front and center, standing where both Adam & Eve; who were stuped down hiding in bushes. ABBA-Father calls out, Adam; where are you? Even Though, he already knew where he was. Adam slowly ascends, with fig leaves - covering his private areas. ABBA-Father says, Adam why are you covered up? He responds, oh I was naked, and ashamed of my nakedness. And ABBA-Father says, Adam who told you - you were naked? Did you eat of the tree? And immediately, Adam points to the woman that came out of him. And Eve turns and says, well the serpent told me all these things. And of course, we know the rest of the story. God made it understood that Eve and the adversary, from that day on-ward, forever, will be at enmity; with each other. Because the serpent caused catastrophic damage to everyone. Starting with our first parents, because we are all seeds (descendants) inside of Adam's sack; waiting to be birthed into existence. So ABBA-Father (of course) cursed the serpent, to make him crawl on his belly, he cursed Eve's belly, and made her and ALL women thereafter have pain (pangs & travail) as unto death - at childbirth, and now he got around to

Adam. He looked at Adam and said - you Lost Everything. For you lost Dominion over Earth. My Earth, that's to be Colonized, and Dominated by You; and All your seeds. Adam, you handed it over to the serpent.   A mere cast - out once upon a time cherub angel, that's now dust. How could you have been so easily persuaded? This was beyond foolish. And hormones & temptation Can't be that overwhelming. Yet, what's done - is done". Be mindful, all the creatures, all the trees & plants, all the fish & the animals, all streams, all hills, all of everything; speak one language. And ALL understood and yielded to Adam, prior. ALL… Well NO MORE.

Christ continues. "And Adam, be it understood; you fell now from Dominion. I didn't give you this Earth. You Adam are the managing agent, prior to all of this. Well, now -Your WORDS are of NO Effect. You've now handed over this planned Colonized world, that I set up - for man to Dominate FOREVER; to the adversary. He only used the serpent's body, because he has NO FORM of his own. He's Nothing more than ashes. Dust. His original name was Lucifer. He was once a cherub angel, but he was cast out from The Kingdom, into the atmosphere; and he has no physical body form. Yet, while he was in Heaven, he was the most beautiful of Angels; that I ever created.   Yet, his beauty went to his head, provoking vanity & conceit; and he self-destructed himself. For self conceit would kill anyone. For it's a consuming fire from within. And now because he has nothing, he's (the prince of the atmosphere), along with his minions; ⅓ of his followers - the fallen angels. And all the while ABBA-Father is explaining all this to Adam, at how he handed Earth over to the adversary; the serpent is Laughing at all these Truths".......

"And suddenly, the serpent stops laughing, looks at ABBA-Father God, slithers and erects that serpent's body to raise up; towering six (6) feet into the air. Standing fully vertical in Eden (The Presence of God), the serpent gazes at Our Heavenly Father".

Christ continues. "The serpent, believing and perceiving to know God's thoughts, says; this is all mine now. You set it up this way.
And then the serpent begins singing the sweetest, most beautiful musical ballad, to Our Heavenly Father. This sudden most beautiful of new

FEDDOR

Melodies springs forth out the serpent's mouth, to God; all while in Eden. And ABBA-Father loves its sound, yet, God knows he is the serpent; that fallen cherub - is a masterful liar. A deceiver and slanderer. And yes, the music is so beautiful, yet; God knows not to take heed. For this is a creature, he had cast out of Heaven. He fell from Heaven like lightning. Dust to the atmosphere. Yet, the music is still beautiful. And now words are spewed. They are sung in the most beautiful of Operatic overtures. For this opus possessed the melodies of three (3) in one sound, of: (Nessun dorma, Ave Maria; and The Lord's Prayer).
I'm sure he's singing to God, saying, in the most Beautiful of lyrics: (You must Now kill them.
These failed mans that you made.
Kill them both.
Because they failed you.
They ate of the tree).
And of course, Eve got on defense, tried to justify herself in saying: he beguiled me. For he told me to eat it, this serpent.
Yet all the while, the serpent is still singing, in the most beautiful Operas.
(You must kill them both.
You are a God of your word.
And your words never change.

You must kill them both.
For Adam broke the Covenant with you.
Eve is a foolish & clueless lass, she's a woman.
Adam FAAAIIIILED YOOOUUUUUU.
For what Adam did was treeaaassssonnn
And treason is to Alwayssss be met with
deeeaaattthhh
Therefore, KIIIILLL TTHHEEEMMMM).
The serpent sang all this in such a beautiful form.
God knowing all of this, instead of Leaning into
what the serpent sang, because he created him,
and he knows of his tactics and tricks; and his
endless talent. So immediately, ABBA-Father
grabbed a lamb; and slew it. And ABBA-Father
placed coats of animal skin on both Adam and
Eve, covering their bodies. He then covered them
with this animal's blood, as a form of atonement.
For the sin (rebellion & disobedience), that they
both made.
The adversary was devastated at this response,
for he was not ready for that wise (defensive)
rebuttal. For the adversary (the serpent), knew the
only thing that could atone for this; was blood.
Clean unblemished blood. For our Heavenly
Father always makes a way (out) of no way".

FEDDOR

Principalities and the Atmosphere

And let's be mindful of what a principality is.
There's the standard definition of principality, yet,
in this sense; principality is a spiritual being.
It is a force oftentimes of wicked or demonic
pretense. For it is a supramundane power, in
conflict with Our Heavenly Father.
Even the dictionary describes them as being
angels in the fifth level of the atmosphere ranking,
and we know that Lucifer and all his minions; fell
from Heaven - to the atmosphere.
And that these creatures, (spirits), exist in the
atmosphere. Yet, these creature spirits are (all)
below man. And ever since that moment in the
garden, there in Eden, God - Our Heavenly Father
had Redemption set in motion, and bought himself
back in the form of Flesh - as Christ on Earth, to
go to the cross; and shed his pure blood.
ATONEMENT.
For ALL sins (rebellion) of man, is covered under
his pure blood, that has restored man; back at
being a Son.   For this is everything that Adam
lost, when he messed up, Christ's placed man
back in control; here on Earth. Dominion once

again. Only for those of us who Believe, and are Believers.

Therefore, Lucifer, (satan, the adversary, the devil), and his minions, are always at work, to keep man from knowing this information; (this TRUTH). And by being at work. He has set up multiple religions as decoys, giving a form of godliness, yet, failing to proclaim the kingdom gospel message, and sonship, and it's been working; unfortunately.

For the adversary has no power, nor authority; over man. Therefore, the only place he can dwell - is in man's thoughts and imaginations. But he is a crafty Beast. For his mission is to bamboozle man, just as he did Adam, and make (man) speak out of his mouth, death & destruction; upon his own self. For words have INCREDIBLE Power. And the adversary knows all too well - how God set up this law of words, over our own lives. Because God gave man back All his Authority, including his words; carrying him. Man has complete Authority and Dominion upon Earth, at whatsoever he requests; he shall have.

Remember that old adage: be careful what you ask for, you might get it. Well, it's true. That's how God set it up. Therefore, these principalities, (fallen angels - minions), along with the adversary;

know this truth as well. So they stay in man's imaginations. And they do so to make him speak out of his own mouth, anything negative, so that this law of words can be used against him, that man automatically self-destructs; from his own words. It's brilliantly evil, and it's been working. Control your Tongue, and control your Life. The Law of WORDS. The adversary has no power nor authority to do anything physically against you, he must get you to do (and say); things against yourself. Incredible…. This is all done at how God set everything up with the Law of Words. The adversary knowing this information, tries to use this to his advantage. Therefore, he wants man never to know this truth, and all these truths, thus mentioned in Our Constitution; the Holy Bible. For when God grants something, a gift or a talent, he never recalls it; for it stays in full effect.

Be ye mindful, these same (fallen) angels and principalities, that have fallen into the atmosphere from heaven, are the same ones that run (mostly) all of the Media; present date. For in Heaven (prior to being cast out), the adversary & his minions would sing, and they would entertain; and they would give praise to Our Heavenly Father.

FEDDOR

And now because they were all up under Lucifer influence, the most beautiful angel of Light, the most captivating of elegance, bamboozled them; and tricked them into being cast out with him. Fallen angels now in the atmosphere. And now in the atmosphere, they THRIVE. Especially in the Entertainment Industry. All of the Airwaves is their Venue. This is their Powerful Influence, and it Works. Not one of them loss any of their talent from heaven. And the media is their prime area of expertise. Therefore, be it known and understood, that they dominate this area and will bamboozle man; if (man) allows. They will woo him over, especially with the entertainment industry, and trick him; winning him over to their side. Faust the term is commonly known, the selling of his soul - to the devil; it's real. Vanity. Captivate him (man) for worldly Glory, riches, and outward praise & applause; of audiences towards him. For the common man is a vain creature, always wanting Glory, and riches. The adversary sees this as an easy target. They even overtly demonstrated this in the cartoon movie "The Little Mermaid". When the sea witch convinces Ariel to give up her fins for a pair of legs, and be human. That she may go to the surface, and find the man that she loves; The Prince - whom she saved from drowning. And the

Sea witch laughs, as she places the spell upon Ariel, giving her legs (as Ariel signs the witch's contract, in agreement for the exchange); yet - losing her voice. You see the adversary is NEVER fair, he's always a LIAR. And the sea witch shouts out of her mouth, "it's too easy, love; and with a Prince". Though this is a metaphor, it is so 100% on point with principalities and how they woo man over. It's completely (Faust) syndrome. Research this (readers).

And all too often it's works, upon those unsuspecting men, (both men and women), unknowingly and unaware; of his devices. He's Smooth.   Subtle. Oh, the devil is real. He's after your Soul, any way necessary.

Therefore, it is so important to understand and to study (the adversary), to know his tricks, and his area of expertise; that you stay always ahead of him.

Yeshua, always spoke to the crowds about the kingdom, and about OUR Kingdom entitlement of entitled Rights, and he always finished off his lectures; about the adversary. How he was kicked out of Heaven, and how to be aware of him; and to not feel inferior to him. Yet, as a cautionary tale to understand he exists, and to know all of his devices, and tricks; and subtlety. Because he has the gift of gab. Very subtle, very smooth; and convincingly conniving. It's not worth it.....

At the very beginning back in Genesis, in our Constitution, we first meet the adversary. First comes God, we meet him, then we meet Adam and later Eve, and then we meet Satan; the devil. His original name was Lucifer, and we meet him at the very beginning. That's how important he is. For he knows God's nature and character, thus, provoking us - in understanding his tricks; and tactics. Though the adversary was kicked out of Heaven, he still possesses all of his intelligence & talent, even though he has no form; except dust particles & ashes.

For Satan's original name was Lucifer, which means bearer of Light. That he once lived in the Kingdom of Our Heavenly Father, prior - in being kicked out; and turned into Ashes.

For the Light Bearer (title), carries the Truth of God. And now because he's out of the Kingdom, he carries the title "the Prince of Darkness", which means - Ignorance; though he possesses all

Intelligence. He is Completely CORRUPTED. And now he uses all his intelligence, now corrupted - and twisted into ignorance, that the unlearned & unknowing man; CAN be deceived. For the adversary knows ALL TRUTHS, but he chooses to change everything over to ignorance and darkness, to confuse man; only if man allows it.

The interesting thing about Lucifer, per the Bible, our Constitution, is that while he lived in Heaven, he was the model of perfection - until wickedness was found in him; and corrupted his ways.

And it says that his heart became proud on account of his Beauty. For this caused him to be cast out, because wickedness was found in him. Much conceit & vanity. For he freely allowed this nature to come in.

I'm sure that when Jesus spoke to the crowds, he advised "Lucifer has come to a horrible end. And he would be no more in Heaven. For he has been reduced down to ashes. From beauty to ashes. And I saw when Michael the Archangel cast him out of Heaven. There was no war. He was cast out of Heaven - instantly. Banished. Gone".

Furthermore, I can see Jesus saying to the crowds, and the people marveling at him; as he spoke about Lucifer. Such as: "Lucifer knew you, before you knew yourself; speaking of his audience. For he was in ABBA - Father God Inner Circle, and he knew all of his intimate details. Therefore, he knew Adam was coming, containing ALL the SEEDS of Human Life; that's to be upon God's Colonized Earth - for Man. And suddenly he chose to become Wicked, and got cast out. Yet, his knowledge and information remained with him, because Our Heavenly Father does not recall; any gifts given. Yet, Lucifer was reduced down to ashes; of no image. Cast into the atmosphere, along with his angels Minions, that have become now demons that followed him. For once upon a time, he had a following".

Talk about Free Will. WOW…

As the old adage says, "keep your friends close, and know them, & keep your enemies even closer; and know them even better".

This stands truer, in dealing with the adversary;
and Principalities.

Hhhmmmm.

Therefore, now knowing this info; look at certain
neighborhoods. Drive through them, and observe
the people. Observe their housing, their yards;
and the general vicinity. Also notice the area
(itself), and the lifestyles, and you will perceive the
environment - by your assessment, usually from
your inner gut feeling; the Governor (the Holy
Spirit) within. This IS REAL…

Get a feel of what type of neighborhood it is.
Observe the present individuals, along with the
individuals frequenting there; (This is notable by a
sense of complacency and conformity). With the
observed information, one can see a notable
lifestyle. And NOW one can see into the
supernatural realm, and notice which principality is
dominating and assigned to that neighborhood;
and community. For these same Fallen minion
angels, are designated to certain areas. And their
mission is to attach, induce and inflict certain
Lifestyles and behaviors; within that vicinity.

Therefore, the attached assignment - tasked upon these principalities to that area, would/will never change, because these Fallen Angel - minions; are on a stronghold (demon) minions Duty.

And on this note, dealing with principalities; look at the school system. Also the political gamut, and the politicians; themselves. Check out their Lifestyles, their Theology, their ethics; and their moral codes. Find out what they stand for. If it doesn't line up With what you believe, and what you stand for, you have to fight hard & diligently; and have change implemented. Or have this person who was voted in, now be voted out. Because whatever they stand for, gets implemented into the community, and into the schools, and this principality now becomes a Constitutional problem and issue; ie: Bussing - Rezoning - Redlining - Redistricting - Gentrification - New Easements, Exclusions Acts, Schools Curriculum - Restrictive Covenants, Housing Discriminatory Acts guised under Eminent Domain and &c… And as Kingdom citizens here on Earth, Sons (that is), we are NEVER to tolerate any form of principality - infringing upon our Constitutional; Sonship of Rights.
For this is Completely Unacceptable…..

THE ULTIMATE POLITICIAN

For we, the Sons of the Most High, are the Legal Citizens of Earth.

In the political gamut arena, a principality (dominating an area), yields much destruction - subtly, reeking havoc unsuspectingly; upon that community.

Dealing with principalities is always evil in nature. They are not Heavenly Angels, on the contrary; these are Fallen Angels.
Their task is to take everything and everyone down, with much subtlety; yet forcefully.
Again, it is that important in understanding the ideology, the theology, and beliefs; of politicians. Because they make things happen, whether good or bad, and your votes determine that influence; or the lack thereof. Therefore, to make change happen you must be present & vocal, making noise; if you don't like how things are going. Especially if their ideology does not line up with yours, make your noise heard.

For we wrestle not against flesh and blood, but against powers, principalities, spiritual wickedness, strongholds, and things in high places; unseen.

Between man on earth, and God in Heaven, there is a massive amount of Spiritual Beings between us; both angels and principalities.

The Angels in the atmosphere are called Heavenly Host. They are massive and mighty. They are massive in numbers, and they are here for our service - as Sons.

There's more going on above your head, than below your feet. God Our Father has given us such great things, to utilize at our disposal; with these Heavenly Host Angel creature-beings.

Both angels and principalities, these things are creatures, they pass around at lightning speed; and soundlessness.

You have the wicked one, the head of the principalities; and they are out there to harm you. And you have the angels from Heaven, the Heavenly host, and they are there to help; and support us.

And these angels (Heavenly host), are also ministering spirits. It says per our Constitution, that when Jesus was finished being tested (in the mountains - tempted by Satan), that the Angels came; and Ministered to Him.

And Lucifer, who once lived in Heaven as an Archangel, was one of God's chosen elite - Inner Circle Angels. And he got kicked out by Michael. Jesus never wrestled against Lucifer, he told the apostles. He said "I saw the devil fall from heaven like lightning".

And angels are created beings. They are NEVER to be worshiped. They are NOT to have monuments, statues, or anything, trying to depict them as an item to be worshiped or prayed to; as a Deity. That was the original problem with Lucifer. He demanded to be worshiped, because he was so beautiful, and could sing well, that conceit found him; and he self-destructed. Literally. He imploded upon himself, disintegrating his physical form; into ashes. And he fell from Heaven into the atmosphere, which is his realm (at present); where he and his minions dwell

The Only Spiritual thing, (person) that can be worshiped, is God Our Heavenly Father; our

Creator.   One must be able to exist (only by one's self), in order to be Worshiped. And that is only God, Our Heavenly Father. All other creatures were created things and beings. Creatures & Beings, (Angels & Man), were either born out of Flesh, or made by God: therefore they/We are sustained by God….

It is impossible to worship anything that was created, for this reason it is ungodly.

Remember, God says - I'm a jealous God; I would not tolerate anything that does not worship me. It's foolish to think that someone, or something, that Our Heavenly Father created; can be worshiped. NO!!! And that was foolish of Lucifer to think that he was to be worshiped. And all because of his Beauty.   He was a created being. God created him, and he wanted the people to serve him.   He thought he could do things better than God, because he was in his inner circle as an Archangel. Well, he was corrupted in his thoughts…

Angels are ministering spirits.

Every man here on Earth has one Angel assigned to him. Two (2) if he is a man of God (Son), for that extra reinforcement.

Keep in mind how powerful these angels are. These are Mighty beings. It took only two (2) Angels to destroy Sodom and Gomorrah, and all its inhabitants

It took only one Angel to roll away the rock that sealed the sepulcher of Jesus. And this was the same Rock, that took 15 mighty soldiers, to put in position, so that the apostles wouldn't be thought to try to steal the body away; and say he was resurrected. Yet, he was resurrected. The Angel of the Lord removed the rock himself, and he did so easily.

You are never to be scared or worried (in life), you have a mighty Force around you. They are invisible, yet, they are ever present, therefore; communicate with them. And if you want them to make themselves visible to you, talk to them, they will briefly; and they will minister to you.
The odd thing about this, is that the same goes for demonic spirits in the atmosphere. There are

foolish people who try to conjure up these spirits. It's real, and they do, making themselves visible and present to them as well; even briefly. And these same conjurers of spirits, have principalities lingering amongst them, for they brought them around; or even within themselves (possessed).

Anyhow, have the ministering Angels of God, talk to you. And they are always assigned to children. God has a special love for children, and their innocence. He will protect them with all might. It will be better for anyone to kill themselves, as it says in the Bible, it would be better to have a millstone tied around one's neck; than to harm one of God's Little Children.

Keep in mind, it was only one Angel (the angel of death) that went through Egypt during Passover; slewing all of the firstborn. One angel, that's how mighty they are.

And remember when Pilate got humbled. Scared. Because Jesus looked at him and said, "all I gotta do is call my father. You have no Authority. I'll just say set loose the Angels, they're standing right there. You can see them. There's 10 to 12 Legion right there waiting to come and take this all out".

But Jesus had love for us. He knew what his Redemptive blood was going to bring us. So he suffered the cross, and tolerated all that nonsenseness; for it had to happen. But he humbled Pilate. And Pilate got scared, because he knew (Christ) was a King.

Angels specialize in strength.
They are Mighty beings, created creature beings.

Just imagine what you cannot see, (the unseen) with your natural eyes; and see with your spiritual eyes - (the supernatural).

It's interesting, the Archangels that surround Gods (we know of three), Michael, Gabriel: and the other was Lucifer. Michael was the warrior, Gabriel was the messenger; and Lucifer was the musician and the Arts. That's why the Arts and the media/entertainment realm is a dangerous scary realm, because that is his expertise. And when he got disintegrated, and cast out of Heaven, because of his own conceit, he fell into the atmosphere, and he's in the airwaves (the clouds); at present. And it's there where he dominates, and forges everything to bamboozle Society,

through the media, social media, tabloids
newspapers, periodicals; Etc.

Archangels are super powerful creatures. Lucifer
was one, but he got cast out. Now he has no
power and never possessed blood, so we are over
him. The only thing he can do, is play in your
imaginations, to make you try (and) talk against
yourselves. Or to do things against yourselves,
and are rightful position as Sons.

Principalities are dangerous (former) Angels.
Because they are known angels to be assigned
over Nations. They have been given an
assignment to cause havoc, especially
Constitutional problems.

And principality (demon spirits) are important, in
their mission for the adversary, for they are the
ones that influence the Laws; and control
societies.

The principalities are the ones that influence a lot
of the printed Publications, that control and run
countries, control laws, and they often harbor
negative influence in society; and the
communities.

THE ULTIMATE POLITICIAN

These principality (demons) are dangerous, because they influence laws, their in the school books influencing children; and people in society. It should be criminal, yet - it's not, that they are in the schools capturing the audience; at a young age.

Very similar to cigarette smoking ads and campaigns. If you notice, they always target audiences younger, and younger, to capture them at a young age; so that they can get them addicted. It's brilliantly subtle, and evil.

And the Education Department is a very sensitive area too. Many principalities control them too. They are governed by principles, and principalities. If you ever notice, the Director of a school is known as a Principle. Hhhmmmm. Not that this is an evil being, yet, oftentimes they are runned by Society; and societal influence.   The Director Principal is just performing a job that is dictated to them.

Case in point how powerful the media is, when you are watching television, look at how politics are being pushed, and events; and elections. Pay close attention to the mindset and ideology of the politician, it's important. Know their Theology, and their ideology. A lot of times, they're pushing a personal (covert) agenda; that a lot of people do not agree with

The thing with principalities is that it is subtle, it is not all of a sudden. It is slow and Insidiously done. They will start trying to influence your mind, getting your mindset to think like theirs. They brilliantly influence your mindset, indoctrinating you, thus provoking change from your ideology; to theirs. It is an Insidious and slow (subtle) way of doing things; very brilliantly. Smart. And almost everything attached to brilliant (and Brilliance), is evil. Because it often takes God out of the equation, thus provoking man to be its basis, and the adversary is the principality; influencing the man's - base.   Pushing man's imagination, because (the adversary) has no form, he has to take on the form of a human body - possessing him with his spirit (way of thinking); in order to push his agenda. And the scary thing is, oftentimes it works.

And with these principalities pushing their agenda, changing man's mindset; it now becomes a stronghold. And a stronghold on your mind gets into your heart. When in the heart, it becomes a lifestyle - and a sin (rebellion); and sinful nature of a community. Remember, as a man thinketh in his heart; so is he. For the principality influencing that community, will demand legislative changes, sent up to have laws changed (and passed); to support this sinful ideology. It's wicked & subtle. Their agenda is not hidden, you can see what's being promoted, and how Society has changed heavily, thus promoting sinful nature (ways); and tolerance. If you notice, the community's agenda under this principality's influence completely avoids and excludes; The Ten Commandments. They toss in the excuse (to avoid the Ten Commandments), mentioning God's grace and mercy.

Yet, Our Constitution, The Bible explains how Christ NEVER came to change the Law; the Ten Commandments. He came to promote the Law. He ONLY added Love into his Doctrine. Letting you know God loves you. He never came to take away the Law, and advise people Grace is now the new law. NO.. Christ said "I came to promote and uphold the law. I just want you to know that God loves you".

Therefore, bringing this info to your attention, on principalities, be watchful and mindful, to what you're listening to & gazing upon; because of its subtle influence. That's the biggest trick of the adversary, and his principalities (demon) minions. You are what you eat. For whatever you take in, that - you become….

And don't be fooled. These same principalities demon minions (devils), their nature is in the church; as well. Another reason why God hates religion, for it's man-made. All subtly done, and hidden; that you don't even notice. But they are there (in the pulpit), preaching these ridiculous jardin and doctrines, promoting music and arts (this is the area of the adversary's expertise); fooling and bamboozling the average congregant.

God hates religion. He would prefer you to stay home, and worship him in your homes, in quiet; and in private. Then to be in the middle of the church, trying to be some (show off), or faked out person; pretending to know and love God. He truly hates (ALL) religion. He never set religion up.

THE ULTIMATE POLITICIAN

It's all from man, and completely man-made.
Religion, God opposes.
God wants man (Son's) to only worship Him.
The adversary knows all of this, so he uses
religion (ALL) as a mighty subtle tool; to control
people. Masterfully done. And it's been working
too. This is the adversary's niche. He's an expert
here, and knows how to win over Society.   So he
wants to take all down, as many as he can,
knowing that they belong to God, he wants to try to
grab them; and snatch them - out of his hands.

For Satan and his minions are rulers of the air.
Therefore, they have access to the airwaves.
Everything coming into the airspace, everything
connected to the media; all to influence Society.

And because they are the rulers of the air, they
have to create precepts for Nations to live by.
These principles and principalities, their precepts;
are not God's (Our Heavenly Father).

And be mindful, sin (rebellion), and a sinful nature,
started off on a personal note; and at a personal
level. Then it becomes a cluster or group of
people, with the same sinful nature/ideology.

Then, they form a committee. Then the committee grows, and they banded together and get (written) legislation backing them. And legislation with this group (this community that grew of like minded - like willed people), gets passed easily, due to the stronghold (principality) has; upon that particular group. Therefore, Society Can't touch them. They are now a force. Again, A STRONGHOLD.......

None of their precepts are God's precepts.

Thus, this becomes a Constitutional issue; and then a Global issue.

It's Brilliantly evil, and subtle.

The adversary is a cunning engineer...

And remember, what's in the community, the schools..

Wow..

How do you get your group's mindset, beliefs, and ideology; into the people - quickest? Though it's somewhat slowly done, but, it gets done. You get the children. So you attack the school system, and its curriculum. And you get your ideology implemented into the curriculum. All promoting this new Constitutional issue.

Hitler did this prior to him becoming president. It was a part of his propaganda push - in getting him elected. And we saw what happened afterwards. It's Horrible.......

THE ULTIMATE POLITICIAN

Be it understood, all of this mentioned, has catastrophic damaging effects on the community/nation; yet - subtly & blatant done.

Remember, the weapons of our Warfare are not carnal but are Mighty. To the pulling down of spiritual strongholds, of powers; and principalities. Fervent prayer (and Faith), to our Heavenly Father, requesting he releases his Archangel Michael (The Warrior); in our defense (as Sons). And the release of our ministering Angels, that we, our families, our households, our communities, and our Nations; are protected.

Remember, Angels are spirits from Heaven above, and demons and demonic forces are principles and principalities; (all fallen angels).
A good example of principalities in the atmosphere, and Angels fighting for our defense, was Daniel's prayer. Daniel's prayer (from Our Constitution), Was Heard immediately by Our Heavenly Father on the first day, and he sent the answer to his prayer; the interpretation of the King's dream. Yet, the angel with the message, fought in the atmosphere, the powers and the

principalities, and after 20 days of fighting, Michael the Archangel (the Warrior); came to his defense. Because the principalities in the atmosphere were great in number, preventing Daniel's answer. For the principalities in the atmosphere formed a stronghold, and a strong force. Remember, they were cast out of Heaven, and now they're angry. They lost everything, due to their rebellion; by listening to the adversary. So they work hard in attempts to prevent any answer to prayers, getting through by our ministering Angels; sent from Our Heavenly Father.

Let me say it again, there's a lot more going on above our head, then that which is going on underneath our feet. For the battles of our Warfare are definitely not carnal But Mighty, to the pulling down of strongholds of powers and principalities, and spiritual wickedness; in high places. Those high places are in the atmosphere, where they have been cast into, (waves & airwaves), affecting the media, the social media realm; causing a strong force and stronghold of demonic influence.

And under this influence, schools promote (and tolerate) immoral Acts. Make it known, to keep it out of the school system, for those are principles attached to principalities; and immoral Acts. For they are set up to handle Constitutional mandates, directed by the State, for principles are somewhat mediators of both society and the state, yet; they are heavily regulated by the State.

It is incumbent upon citizens (son's), being part of Boards and Committees in the school system; advocating for our Children. As well as within your Communities, making it known of certain precepts and ideologies from groups within your community, that don't line up with yours; nor that they reflect those of Our Heavenly Father's original PRECEPTS.   And this goes for the schools, and the government, make it known; be vocal.   The squeaky wheel gets the oil.   Make your vote and voice count, and get those people either voted out; or tossed out. Otherwise, get your family out of that location - of Tolerance.   For once it becomes a Constitutional sin (rebellion) against God's precepts, the principality of that region is then a stronghold.

It doesn't matter if you have children in that school system or not, you make your claim and your words known; the squeaky wheel really does - get the oil.

For the Bible (our Constitution) says, we (Sons) are to be Disciples in the Nation.

You don't have time to allow principalities to Run away with your children, and get a stronghold on their minds; at their young impressionable ages. This is nonsenseness.   You take control and authority over the situation, and get involved.

Angels are proof that there is much going on in the world above us, that we cannot see; with our natural eyes.

Angels were created to be ministering Spirit to those of us (Son's), that are heirs of Salvation.

Angels warn us of God's justice and judgment.

And take warning from the Angels, and the Holy Spirit. For if God didn't spare the Angels that he cast out of Heaven, and he created them; how much more will he not spare you. Therefore, take heed. For God loves us, and he wishes that for none of us - to perish.

THE ULTIMATE POLITICIAN

You have to obey God. For God loves us, but God is faithful to his own word. For God deals with sin, and he deals with sin seriously. He does not tolerate sin. People often say, and confuse his Grace, to be a covering for sin; and sinful ways. NO.. Grace does not cover Sin. Sin is Sin. Christ did NOT die on the cross to give us a license to sin. God deals with sin seriously. Yet, God also has lots of love for us. Therefore he gives us ample opportunities to always correct things that have or has - gone wrong. Remember, sin is rebellion. Sin means Rebellion. And when you Rebel, having a sin or sinful nature; God deals with that. He brings to your mind (attention) - areas to get it right. That's what the Holy Spirit does, he quickens in your spirit; things that need to be correct. For God chastens those whom he loves.

Angels give us two choices, as we know from the cartoons, we can choose to be on God's side; or on the adversary's side. God being Light (knowledge and truth), the adversary being Darkness (ignorance and Lies). And those that are on the adversary's side, are utterly cast down.

FEDDOR

And one of the main problems in society, where principalities get to have a great influence; is because the Father is not in the home. And if he is in the home, he does not know his proper Role. For if he is not guiding his family under the influence of God, he doesn't even have the directions, or know; what he is doing. He is head of household. Fathers are very important. The Covenant was with man (Adam).

The Seed

Through the Father, the head of the household, is the foundation; and the covenant for the family is established. For this reason, nothing happened to Eve when she bit the fruit, for the Covenant was not with her; it was with Adam. Fathers (males) are that important, that God established a covenant with them/us. For this reason, we possess ALL the seeds. And we have the character, (the image) of God. The woman is a nurturer. She is an incubator of God's purpose. The man possesses God's seed and character. Fathers are that important. Therefore, Fathers stop running off from your responsibilities. And women, stop chasing him away; and build him up.

Women, you have a strong position in life. You can Build UP (the man) and encourage him, as Eleanor Roosevelt did for her husband Franklin, who became President, and Eleanor - the Greatest First Lady that Ever existed; And she was of the Nobility - the Aristocracy. Or Women, you can let your tongue be possessed by a Jezebel spirit, and tear Him Down; and chase him OFF. Which will cause destruction and havoc in the home, and then in the community, and then in society; and the Nation. Thus, causing all these different principalities to take hold, and have a strong hold over a nation, that could have been prevented, by having a Man with a Purpose (VISION); in the HOME.

For the sole purpose of the principalities is to cause DESTRUCTION. Therefore (all parties), wake up and comprehend how important the role of the Father - in the Home; IS.

And Fathers, be a good Father, and be like King David. For King David told his son Solomon, while upon his Deathbed, he said "Son, show yourself a man, and Keep the Laws of Our Heavenly Father, and walk in all his ways. Keep his Commandments, and show your Love to the Lord, and walk in his ways; and upright". King David, gave such a strong speed to his son Solomon. God truly Loved David.

And as Jesus gave instructions, while speaking to the crowds. That we are always to be in constant communication with Our Heavenly Father. For this prevents principalities, from crossing over; into our lives - freely. They will always try, but he will not have free access, if you are in constant communication; with Our Heavenly Father. All you (the Son) have to do is talk to ABBA- Father, pray, sing songs of praise; and thanks. And when we pray, we are always to use the Lord's Prayer, (Our Father Who Art in Heaven, Hallowed be thy name. Thy kingdom come, thy Will be done, on Earth; as it is in Heaven. This is proof that God had planned to Colonize Earth, and make it mirror Heaven. Man was never to go to Heaven. Earth was colonized to mirror Heaven, and for man to possess it and dominate it; FOREVER....

In reference to Heaven, man should concentrate on the Clouds of Witnesses (Per our Constitution, in the book of Hebrews), where the souls go prior to returning to Earth; those of us who are Sons. For Heaven is for God, Our Heavenly Father. Earth is for man. Man's soul, and his Spirit, is to possess Earth Forever. ABBA-Father made us a Beautiful Earth.

We, (Man) are to fill the Earth, with the culture of Heaven; that is God's strategy.

FEDDOR

Remember a Kingdom is a country occupied by a King. And the citizens are acting like the King (Colonization), possessing a mirrored image; of Our Heavenly Father.

For a Kingdom is a culture, Not a religion.

For Earth is to be filled with the culture of the Kingdom of Heaven.

Again, God created man to have dominion over Earth forever. And for us not to live in Heaven, for Heaven is for God.

For God sent us (man) to this earth, to occupy Earth; with his image. Image, meaning - his character and his characteristics, and to have the culture of Heaven; here on Earth.
And be mindful, God did not allow anything to grow on Earth, nor did rain appear on Earth, until he created man; to manage everything. The moment man showed up on Earth, rain appeared. Because God gave perfect instructions to Adam, to have dominion over the Earth. And Adam was to manage all of this, and be the Governing agent here upon this Earth; dominated by man. That is when God allowed rain to show up, and for the

earth to become fruitful; and multiply its seeds. Because he had his Covenant partner, managing agent, upon the Earth; and that was Adam. And unfortunately to say, until Adam messed everything up with his treasonous act; and relinquished everything over to the adversary. Yet, God already had redemption set in motion, with his son coming (to Earth) to restore man back to his rightful position, here on Earth, and in right standings with God; through his son Jesus Christ - Yeshua to be OUR Redemptive savior.

Thinking realistically, it had to have been very difficult, extremely difficult - during slavery times, here in America, for an Enslaved person; to be a believer. Yet, somehow or another, it took hold. The enslaved caught hold of spirituality. For they always sung those Heaven bound songs, All Hope from the bondage and chains of oppression. That is very common, for anyone that is oppressed. To think, speak and dream - on a higher level; that is not in their present physical realm. I'm even sure that the Israelites - too, while they were in bondage, sang songs of the afterlife in Glory; or a form of Paradise.

Yet, Heaven is only for God, and Earth was made and created for man, permanently; and for our Spirit to dominate. Heaven, and the concept of man going to Heaven; often came from bondage. Again, Earth was made for man to have dominion over, and his spirit to live upon it; Forever.

Yeshua speaking to the masses
Repent means "CHANGE YOUR THINKING"

In order to change your life, you first must change your hearing; and what you're taking in. Again that old adage: you are what you eat, is both literal and figuratively. If you're going to take in trash, you're going to become trash. If you take in any good things, that's what you become. For your mind, your eyes, mouth, and your ears; are entry ports to your soul. Use them wisely.

Fathers in the household:
The best thing a father can do to his newborn child, and to his wife and family, is to love his wife. That the child may see the transference of love, and learn his position and purpose, as a positive male; and head of household.

The duty of a Father is to love the children.

Fathers do not allow your children to become wayward, for it is written - a child left alone brings his parents to Shame.

As a Father you are to set standards, give correction, set values; and morals to your children. They need your financial support, yet - more importantly, they need your love and attention. A Father's love, attention, and kindness is everything; the adversary and principalities CAN'T touch this BOND.

A real Father teaches his household the word of God, our Constitution.

Father's, Do Not measure your standards of Fatherhood based off of your own Father (or lack thereof); experience. For if your own natural Father was not that image of a Godly man in your life, then he missed an important step in bringing you up. Instead, turn to God's love, and his moral standards; based off of Our Constitution. Therefore, you have to base your Fatherly standards off of Our Heavenly Father. For Our Heavenly Father has nothing but Love for us. And he will withhold NOTHING from us. This is how we (as natural Father's) are to be with our (own) children, as he is with us.

In order to know good you have to know God. Therefore to be a good Father, you Must have God in the midst of everything you say and do, so that your children will mirror what they see; displayed from you. For Love is a Learned Behavior, as EVERYTHING in life is Learned, except for blinking and fight/flight (innate - defense mode); natural responses.

Our Constitution - the Bible says that the Father corrects and chasens the child. Bring up a child in the way he should go, and when he is older; he shall not depart from it.

If you love your child, you will correct him. A child always wants proper correction, especially from the Father. It is at those times he knows that the father cares, and loves him; and will not allow him to do whatever he chooses.

The salvation of a Nation, and your community, starts in your household; Fathers take heed.

Every naturally born son should be able to say - I am a Son of Our ABBA-Father God.

Children receive the philosophy of life from people, (the concept), therefore, make sure that the people they are (subjected to), are first and foremost correct in their ways; & lifestyle. Otherwise, they are receiving wrong information; and philosophy. And if things have gone amuck, Fathers must access - and see; how they in particular - have failed the child. To prevent this, Fathers stay Present & Vigilant.

FEDDOR

A Wicked concept that exists, is that the child/children can emancipate themselves; from their parents. There are some instances where this is necessary (abuse, and so forth), yet - some children wish for complete freedom from their parents; because they think they are grown. It's a spiral downhill, don't allow this; the child is clueless.

This is unacceptable. The child must live by the standards of moral and values you've set in that household. Especially when the household is Guided by a Father, who is focused with a vision; for the Family. The adage, listen to your parents and you'll live longer; this comment is so true.

As parents, Fathers especially, have a responsibility to bring the children up properly.

It's part of Father's Duty. He is to instruct and teach his children, giving them guidance, morals, values; and directions.

Father's, it is impossible to instruct, if you have not been instructed. Otherwise, if he has been properly guided (himself), under good Biblical tutelage in the word, our Constitution; makes for a ton of difference in the Family Institution.

THE ULTIMATE POLITICIAN

Yeshua, The Ultimate Politician - spoke always to the people, and the crowds, to be on my side of Our Heavenly Father; and his Precepts - the Ten Commandments. Yet, the Chief Priests and Pharisees hated him. They thought that this was pure blasphemy.

For the fear of the Lord is the beginning of wisdom. Understanding that there are consequences, but too - also there's Love. Therefore comprehend God's love, and fear his Wrath; and stay on the righteous side.

Fathers teach children the Commandments of God.

Fathers, always encourage your children, and warn them of things necessary to be aware of.

Don't threaten the children, warn them to live their lives; worthy of God.

When you warn a child they will receive the warning as love, and care; from a father.

FEDDOR

And bear in mind that the seed has authority over the scene. Though the ground needs the seed to work, the seed still has the authority over the ground.

And the dirt that the seed is placed in, often puts pressure on the seed, to pull out the fruit that is contained within. This metaphor is intended both literally and figuratively.

For the steps of a righteous man are divinely ordered, by our Lord, that all things work out for our good.

Hebrews 12 goes into details on the seed relationship of goodness, between a Father and Son.

For the Bible, our Constitution, says father love your children; and do not provoke them to Wrath. Yet, instead - train them always in the way they should go.

And women, it is in your best interest to latch onto a Good man; especially a man after God's Heart. For this is a man with a Purpose, and vision. He has a covenant attachment, with the Most High.

A good woman can build up a man, and make him incredible. And when she comprehends that he is a man of God, of substance, she can build him up knowing he's a Son; and she recognizes his Covenant agreement.
An example of a good woman that built her husband up in the secular realm, was Eleanor Roosevelt.

And woman, stay away from the Jezebel spirit. Neither have Jezebel spirited friends, you know who they are. Because that is an evil Wicked spirit, that is easily rubbed off upon, and it will contaminate you; and your household. It is a cursed spirit. You can read much on this reading, independently, by this self-same author's work; Posterity.

Just a reminder, the Holy Spirit (the Governor); is a person. He is the personality of God. The Holy Spirit is described to us per our Constitution) as "HE", meaning he is in fact a person.

Proving this truth of the Holy Spirit says that he has emotion. He can grieve. He can also talk to you. He can also teach you, if you feed him information. For he is always known to recollect (in your spirit) things you have learned, refreshing it to your memory; at times when needed. He is not able to furnish you with new information that you did feed (supplied) him with.

The Holy Spirit is peaceful and orderly. There is no disorder with him. He is known as the comforter, and a source of comfort.

And on this note, dealing with Charisma - which is derived from the word charismatic (meaning gifts of the Spirit); for this gift comes directly from the spirit of God.

We are the body of Christ. We are the Temple of the church. We are the Holy Spirit's (the Governor) Temple, this is his sanctuary.

Be it understood, that all good gifts come from Our Heavenly Father; this is what Charisma is. Charisma means gifts of the Holy Spirit.

God gave us Angels to watch over us, to minister to us. We (Son's) are to tell our Angel to protect us, when we go places. To bring us any necessary finances, to take care of us and our household; and they must do so. They have been assigned to attend to us. God's Sanctified people. Sanctified meaning set apart, for we are Son's.

And in our Constitution, the Bible, says that we were made in the image of God, which means (not his physical image), but his moral image, his character, his ideology; and his charisma meaning character (gift of the Spirit).

For everything made by Our Heavenly Father - God is good, as he said in his word; in Genesis.

For God created everything out of nothing. Yet, when he made (Man/Male), he didn't create man, he formed him out of what already existed; the dirt from the ground. He created the dirt. He Formed Man. And when he formed man, he gave man his Charisma, His image, and then God breathed in man's nostrils; and gave him life. This emphasizes the Covenant Bond with man & God. Man - being Adam, the first man/male, our original father; on Earth.

FEDDOR

And God named the first man/male Adam. For Adam is a man. And Man is a Spirit, that possesses a Soul; and lives in a Body.
For the Soul consists of the WILL of a man, the mind of a man; and the emotions of a man.

And when God breathed into Adam's Spirit, it gave him life; to his soul.

That which is born to flesh is flesh (such as animals), but that which is born of a Spirit - is of the Spirit. For Man has a spirit, with the characteristics of God.

The purpose and the power of the Family, and the role man here upon Earth, is all for the purpose of the Kingdom - from our Heavenly Father; and the Kingdom Concept (of Son's on Earth).

And dealing with family (spouses) - you must qualify for marriage. You must take classes, and get approved. For it should be difficult to get married, and obtain a marriage license; (yet it's not). Marriage is a very serious Institution, ordained by God.

Keep in mind, the Bible - Our Constitution says, my people are destroyed for a lack of knowledge. For the Devil is the author of confusion and ignorance (darkness). This is his realm of expertise, to keep people lacking information and knowledge. Keeping man in darkness. Yet Christ is light (knowledge, intelligence, wisdom & understanding); to man.

For the Bible says, by knowledge and wisdom is a house built. Therefore the most important key, in the Kingdom Concept, is the Family life; and Relationships.

We (Son's/Believers) are Kingdom citizens. We must submit to the King, upon his Colonized Earth. And we must mirror His Heavenly kingdom, here on Earth.

We MUST live by our Original Country/Kingdom's Precepts (the Ten Commandments), being that we are representatives; of our Heavenly Father's Kingdom. And be Ambassadors here on Earth, the Colonized territory from our Heavenly Father, maintaining all of his precepts; and his directives.

FEDDOR

Therefore as a Kingdom citizen from our Heavenly Father's Kingdom country, we are to live by higher values; and standards,

Keep in mind Christianity is a religion, and you can do almost anything under the pretense of religion. Yet, these religious standards are not acceptable by our Heavenly Father. For the Kingdom of God is a country & a Government; NOT a religion. And we as SONS are to live by higher standards, governed and sanctioned by the precepts given us (originally); from our King and Heavenly Father.

Therefore, the concept of Family is so important; for it is the oldest institution ordained by God.

For society can point most of its Solutions and crisis of National problems, to the restoration of Family. The family is the key to a stable Nation.

Society is a reflection of what's going on in the family.

The purpose of the family is to secure Society.

Find your purpose in life. This is achieved by talking directly with the one who made you, our creator; Our Heavenly Father.

For whomever you have a relationship with, there you find your purpose…

The male's purpose is to stay in God's presence, and to preserve his presence of God (Eden); in the presence of God. And to bring other males into the presence of God, for the Covenant is with us/Males; for we possess the SEEDS of Our Heavenly Father.

And the man/male figure in the home, number one assignment and purpose; is to keep God's presence - Eden in the house.

For God said all of this to Adam in the beginning, immediately after creating him; and giving him dominion over everything. All instructions given, prior to Eve's arrival on the scene. God told Adam, never touch the tree in the midst of the garden. All instructions were only given to Adam. No instructions from God were ever given to Eve, because the Covenant was not with her; it was with Adam.

FEDDOR

Per Genesis, when God created Adam he did so by forming him from the dirt that now already existed, which he had already created. Yet, he formed Adam from the ground. Whereas with Eve, (the female), she was part of Adam, but he (God) didn't form her, instead - he BUILT her directly out from Adam; for she (Eve) was BUILT from him. And though God formed Adam, he built Eve directly from Adam. Yet, he had to make a few adjustments, to prepare her to cultivate the seed of Adam, and of all the seeds Adam has within; for Every Generation thereafter. All intentionally done, so that God's purpose of man always being in his presence (God/Eden) here upon this Colonized Earth, which is to be MAN'S Perpetual home; for his Spirit Forever.

And after God built Eve, he brought her before the presence of Adam; and presented her to him. Because God didn't want Adam to be alone. Yet, God never gave Eve to Adam, God only presented her to Adam, and Adam began communicating with her; and forming their bond (wink-wink).

And be mindful, the female who came out of Adam (Eve), Adam then said "I will call you WOMAN.

For you are formed out of me, meaning a Man with a WOMB".

This answers current discussions and debates, of things going on in today's society; about Gender. I will not go into gender identity, that is something personal going on - in that individual's head; remember - Principalities..   Let's just take it all back to the beginning, when God made Adam and Eve; and that sums it all up...

And just a reminder, sin means Rebellion. Rebellion goes against any of the original precepts, the Ten Commandments; which has Never changed. Even Societal Laws are based off of the Ten Commandments; both then and present date. For these are the Laws of the Nations.   And when one goes against the Laws (Sin/Rebellion), this is not allowed; nor tolerated. For God deals with it.   It is for this reason man has made (INVENTED) his own religion. Because he said these original precepts that were given to us from God are a bit too strict. Therefore, let us create (Invent) RELIGION, as a Celestial substitute; and lessen the burdens of these precepts.   That

FEDDOR

RELIGION might make our lives more comfortable, under our own terms.
This proves that God is against religion.
For man implemented religion, because he is often in Rebellion; possessing a sinful nature..
For religion is the worship of a deity, with certain rituals, customs, and beliefs, attached and Associated; to only that particular religion.
Religion causes separation, and Division in society.
Religion always causes Wars.
God is love. War, Division, and separation; are NOT in his vernacular.

As a man and a Son of God, OUR purpose in life is to have dominion over Earth; and dominate it. Dominion meaning Sovereignty. Absolute Power and Control. Fulfilling God's WILL, as a Son. For here on Earth, the Son's have Complete Sovereignty.
God's Kingdom purpose is to fill the planet Earth with the culture of Heaven. No principality can prevent this, for that was the reason in going to the Cross was about. Restoring man back to his Purpose.

We (Sons) are rulers for God, here on Earth. For Christ restored us, renewed our mind as Sons, and made us rulers here on this Earth; Forever. And WE were created to dominate everything, here upon this Earth. The plants, the fish, the trees, the animals, the bugs, the air, the wind, the ocean, God gave us Sonship; for we are the descendant seeds of Adam. Given Dominion to dominate.

We (man-Sons) to our Heavenly Father, are never to be dominated; we are the dominators.

And Yeshua came to Earth to show us (man/Sons) of God how we are to live here on Earth, mirroring the culture of Heaven; and in character as Our Heavenly Father.

And when Yeshua was here, he went into Towns and Villages in his region, healing the sick, casting out demons, and relieving the oppressed, because there is no oppression of any form, neither is there any lack of anything; nor negativity - in the Culture of Heaven. And Yeshua came and restored man's thinking (repent), to this Realization.

And as a man/Son, we hate being ruled over or dominated, by anyone; or anything. We don't like anything having any form of control over us, that's why we dislike borrowing from the banks (ie., understanding who controls that lending system - hmmm); thus - making man a slave. For debt is the other form of slavery. Therefore as Son's of God, we have Faith & believe - he will pay off everything; supernatural. For the Holy Spirit (the Governor - within), will guide us and instruct us; in how to use much wisdom.

Yeshua would advise the crowds, "you are blessed by my Father. Follow after me and my teachings, and receive your rightful due heritance; it's yours already. Your inheritance is entitlement in having dominion over the world. You are an Ambassador, Sanctified by your Heavenly Father".

As Sons from the Kingdom (Life), and Ambassadors, we were sent by the Government of Heaven, to represent - as being an Agents of Heaven; here on Earth. And by being an Agent/Ambassador, everything is taken care of for us Sons; by our Heavenly Father. Therefore, as an Agent/Ambassador Representative; our Heavenly Father takes care of our every whim. For we are to represent him in every form, and the Culture of Heaven. We are to have NO Opinions of our Own, we say only what the King and Creator; has Already Stated. And we/Son's are to instruct man, (who may be in Rebellion - sin), in a kind and loving way; to change his thinking and habits (repent). For Rebellion brings forth (darkness - ignorance), sickness, and lack, yet; our Father possesses none of these things. For He is Light Wisdom & Abundance, in ALL Things; and likewise are We as Son's.

Remember, man fell from Dominion on Earth - that he was given the assignment to dominate. Man did NOT fall from Heaven, for man never lived in Heaven. Man was formed and created, here on Earth, this real estate that he was told by God to dominate; this is man's Dominion for his Spirit forever.

The biggest issue that occurred when Adam fell from Dominion, was the adversary was allowed to play in his thoughts and imaginations; inflicting him with self-doubt. Provoking Adam to think he was Not already as God. We (man/Sons) are little Gods, below the Most High. Yet, the adversary

FEDDOR

Bamboozled him and Eve, convincing them - if they ate of the tree of knowledge they would be like God; or even better. That was a foolish and treasonous mistake. Self-doubt

Yeshua came to give us (back) our own self image. Because the average man has an identity problem, that's what the adversary took from him. Self-doubt. The average man doesn't know who he is. And then slavery (enslavement), and other forms of oppressive bondage (ie., Debtor prison, penal colonies, assisted migration, convict leasing penal system, debt, student loans imprisonment, human trafficking, &c.), came along by the adversary and principalities, shattering man's self confidence; that he is supposed to be a Son. All of this has occurred throughout history, Society (the Principality System); inflicting Self Doubt upon man. Yet, Yeshua restored man back to his proper place and identity, giving man back the character of God. The character of God is his personality, and his know-how; and that we have dominion over all of this. Man MUST step up and realize this FREE GIFT of God's love and Restoration.

Yeshua, The Ultimate Politician was WELL received when he was here by Society; excluding those High Priests. For the people received him, and they saw who they are to be in God. When they saw Yeshua, God In the Flesh, and was shown & instructed on how to be little Gods here upon this Earth, all under the Most High, that all of the crowds throughout Society - loved it; yet the High Priests hated it. For the majority of their congregants abandoned the Priests teachings, and followed after Yeshua. As well as many of the pagan Romans, followed after Yeshua.

And now, these High Priests conspired to have Yeshua killed, for he was affecting their revenue; and they needed him gone - permanently. They hated Yeshua, because he was giving these people (the masses) back their identity, of Sonship - with God; here upon the Earth. These religious leaders and High Priests hated this, because they were able to manipulate man, keeping his mind bound & oppressed (self-doubt); all under the guise of Religion. Yet, Yeshua was setting them free; advising that religion was to NO Avail.

And Yeshua instructed society of what they are to do, and how they are to live, by our Constitution; the written word of God.

Thus, all said by Yeshua, was in conflict with these High Priests, provoking them into bringing bogus charges against him for his crucifixion. Unbeknownst to them, this was all part of God's plan.

For when the crowd heard and observed all the things Yeshua said, and the miracles performed, and were astounded when he advised they too can do all this and more; they loved him all the more. For his words resonated within their spirit, and they grasped their identity in God; and knew all that he said was completely TRUE.

And Yeshua informed them - never to look at their human self and think that this life they live is normal. Instead, he told them to look at their inner Spirit, (the unseen), and see all that you can do (in the Supernatural); that the human cannot.

And the reason why all the different religious (man's search for God) groups exist, is because man is constantly looking for Heaven. All because man is tired of being dominated here on Earth, by his brother; and all these other outside forces. Therefore, to escape their present reality, man envisions Heaven; as being their relief & Escape. But Man was not made for Heaven. He is to dominate Earth, where he belongs. And this is difficult for man to comprehend, due to all the evils in the world (presently); dominating him. Thus causes him to look for an escape, out of here, not comprehending - here is where he is to stay, as a Son; on this Colonized Earth - from Heaven.

And when I speak of man hates being dominated & oppressed, I'm talking about the Banking systems, the working class system, the Caste system in society worldwide, Reparations to the descendants of American Enslavement - Along with a Public Apology, reparations to the descendants of the Indigenous re-education program and an apology, the various abuses from the church - and churches, the Civil Rights Laws - Violations & Issues, &c, and also the various infirmities, most have been bought on because of these other dominating factors, wearing down man; and stressing him out.

Man is supposed to be in control of himself, possessing dominion, and that all of his spoken words; are to carry him throughout Life.

Man/Son has been instructed, here on Earth, to act like God; which is what Yeshua instilled in us. For we possess Our Heavenly Father's image (character), therefore, sober up; and let's act like him.

And elaborating a little more in this capacity, a small note on the Rapture per this author, and others too; believing as such. For Once Upon a Time, I too believed this Celestial event; to be taking place. Yet, much research has caused me to change my thinking (repent); on this Rapture moment.

My research has proven that this is something that has been promulgated by high level Jesuit Priests from the 16th Century, and later in the 1960's some new edition international Evangelical Bibles; started proclaiming this promulgated doctrine - as fact. Advising, it will be taking place soon, and many (alleged theologians) jumped on this bandwagon, believed; and preached this doctrine. It is nothing more than Futurism. The Bible (our Constitution) speaks about how, and when; Jesus will return. Even though the word says, there will be wars; and rumors of wars. And things happening throughout the World, ie., earthquakes, calamities, Nations Rising against Nations; that Paul had mentioned in Thessalonians. Jesus said, in our Constitution, I will come after ALL men, in

ALL Nations, and ALL tongues; know about the KINGDOM. The Kingdom of God's Doctrine message. And understanding that the Bible is ALL of OUR Constitution. And ONLY then, after ALL men know this TRUTH; that's when I will come. For God loves people. And that they are to know that they are entitled to everything mentioned in their Constitution; the Bible. And how God colonized Earth, that it is to mirror Heaven. And that man is to have dominion over this Earth, this large piece of beautiful Real Estate. Until then, I will NOT come. And as you can see, many nations still don't know about the Kingdom; and the Kingdom of God's Doctrine Message; (that's the GOOD NEWS MESSAGE of Christ). For it is upsetting that the Christian Church has failed, and been failing, by NOT preaching this Kingdom Doctrine message; of the Good News. Since there are numerous religions, they have been failing too. Therefore, Preach the kingdom; and all of your entitled inherent rights. Teach all that Adam lost, and that Christ restored man back to his rightful Position, as a Son; and that God will always Supply his needs. For Our God is a loving God, he created us; he's OUR Author..

FEDDOR

The message of the Bible (our Constitution) is about a King and his Kingdom, and his Royal Family, us as Sons; here on Earth.

Our Heavenly Father has many names, and one of them is Adonai; which is Hebrew meaning Lord Master.

In reference to religion, it is man's (secular) attempt in finding the Kingdom. God never implemented religion.....

It is most important that you know your Constitution, and that you are loyal to the correct doctrine; and that you are guided properly. For many people are fooled by many fabled Doctrines.

Sons, stay mindful - that Duty and Decorum is the Protocol for us, from the Kingdom. As Sons here upon Earth (our domain), that we have dominion over.

The adversary, is anything contradictory to the Kingdom of God; for he is the author of ignorance. And religion, is contradictory to the Kingdom of God. Religion, was never implemented by God;

Our Heavenly Father. Religion really throws people off.

And the scary thing is that religion is a very powerful Institution. It has a very powerful Spirit. More powerful than any of the other demon Spirits upon Earth.

Therefore, to have success in the Kingdom requires much knowledge. One must engage in constant enlightenment spiritually, much prayer, and much fellowship with the Holy Spirit; the Governor. For the Holy Spirit dwells within Our Earthly Temple human body.

Jesus came to bring a living Kingdom to Earth for us, and to have this Kingdom attached to us - Forever.

A Kingdom is the manifestation over the world, the territory is the domain. For the world is called the Government, the Government's influence over its territory.

FEDDOR

Christ says your inheritance is the Kingdom, that was prepared and established for you; from the beginning of the Earth's creation.

And all the Laws that were written, is to protect the interest of a Country.

As the Bible says, all things work together for my good. For I have appointed you personally as representatives of the Kingdom of Heaven, here on Earth; the colonized mirrored image of the Kingdom of Heaven. Us, Sons - have this Authority.

Always reflect on how Jesus instructed us, that when we pray - we are to say "Our Father, who lives in Heaven - Holy is thy (your) name. Thy (your) Kingdom come. Thy (your) Will be done, On (this Colonized) EARTH as it is in HEAVEN. Give us (Ambassadors/Sons) this day all things necessary for the Kingdom Purpose and our provisions (daily bread). And forgive us of ANY Rebellion (sin/trespasses), and that we forgive those who trespass (sin/problematic) against us, that we have no ought against our brothers. And lead us not into temptation of rebellion (sin), and deliver us from evil, the snares of the adversary and principalities. Amen".

For the prayer of the "Our Father", is the prayer to turn; Earth into Heaven.

That's how Jesus/Yeshua told us to Pray.....

With us as Kingdom citizens (Sons), on Earth in society; we stand out. And by standing out, everybody should always wonder, where we are from, because we talk and think differently; than others (the masses). As Son's, we are on another plateau in our dialogues. We are to be influencers, advising others - that they too can be part of this Colonized Kingdom Citizenship; for this is your Rightful Inheritance.

And just as Jesus told Pilate, when asked "where are you from"? Jesus said "my Kingdom is not of this world". We too are to advise in a like manner.

And advise others, those inquiring, "I am under the influence of my Heavenly Father; and the Kingdom of Heaven.

For the Kingdom of Heaven is the Government, the King and his influence upon the Earth - for his

Sons; and for his sons to act like him upon this Earth. For we, the Sons have dominion over this territory - Earth; Forever.

And since we are Sons, we have Angels assigned to us, at our disposal; to cater to our every whim. For God put the Angels here to minister to us, to protect us, and to work with us, and do all we ask; as we perform Kingdom Purpose Protocol.
I like how the Nobles say of the Aristocracy, that the purpose of the Prince is always "Duty and Decorum". On this note I say ditto, to our Heavenly Father kingdom's purpose; here upon this Colonized Earth.

We/Sons, are to take on the Kingdom Concept of Kings. For we are Sons, Kings, we are all under the Most High, those of us who Proclaim Our Heavenly Father (ABBA-Adonai-God), as our Savior & Lord; from all that Adam lost.

Again, the message of the Bible, Our Constitution, is about a King and his Kingdom, that came down to Earth and Colonized it with his familial Royalty, deeming us his Royal Sons (HEIRS); to be here Forever - in his STEED.

Much has been explained in great detail here. I query the reader to do further research and acquire enlightenment as to the reason they are here, upon this Colonized Earth - For God's Heaven; and recognizing their true Purpose. Hopefully you shall get a revelation that you are a Son, if you're not one already.

Furthermore, we should understand and know the actual Covenant agreement symbol God gave Noah. It was a bow in the sky, going through the clouds. A beautiful multicolor bow.

After God destroyed the Earth, via the flood, Our Heavenly Father made a covenant agreement with Noah and said, "I shall never destroy Earth, nor man ever again; especially in this form. And here now is my Covenant agreement with you Noah. I set forth my beautiful multicolored bow in the sky, that when you gaze upon it, you know that - that is my agreement. I shall never do this again".

That said, when we (present date) see this bow (rainbow) in the sky, we are to recognize, and remember this covenant agreement between God

and Noah; which STILL affects us NOW.
Therefore, this is a Sacred and Sanctified symbol,
to that Covenant; let's keep it that way. We ALL
are direct descendants to Noah, and of course
from Adam too. Yet, since God started everything
over again, with man upon Earth; we are all seeds
of Noah. And when we look in the sky, and
observe after a heavy rain that bow - in the sky, we
know that it's God saying; "I Shall not destroy
Earth". God is just reminding man of this
Covenant agreement.

Though science will say it's all from the gasses.
Yet, we the BELIEVERS know, this bow, according
to our Constitution, our Bible states this God sworn
covenant agreement to Noah, that he shall never
destroy man ever again, in this form - and placed
this beautiful image; in the sky.

Therefore, let us always recognize….

And on this note, and that of the Rapture:

The rain came immediately when Noah finished
his assignment, and shut the door of the Ark.
Though he warned the people and told them to
come, yet; they scorned him. The animals, guided
by their spirits, came automatically; and entered
the Ark. And the moment Noah shut the door of
the Ark, God sent the rain. For Noah's assignment
in constructing the Ark, was completed.

Understanding this, Christ will come AGAIN (in the End), when we the sons (the Saints upon the Earth) finished preaching the Kingdom of God message, as a testimony to All Nations; and to all ethnos. And Yeshua advised "once that is completed I will come, until then - I'm not coming back". Man must be fairly warned, and told about the Kingdom of God's Doctrine, and all of their entitled rights and benefits, so that man can make a conscious decision to either be with Our Heavenly Father - as a Believer; or choose not to listen.

Therefore, don't be deceived by people running around preaching and shouting - Jesus is coming, Jesus is coming; Jesus is coming. Instead, adhere to what Our Constitution says, per Matthew 24, the Kingdom of God's message, to be preached to All Nations, all kindreds; and all tongues.

FEDDOR

Your life as a Son is to line up with the precepts God has given us.

For our Heavenly Father's yoke is an easy one. Therefore, give your burdens to him, and stop trying to carry the cares of the world on your own shoulders; it's impossible. Give it to God, let him handle it for you. We have the Holy Spirit (the Governor), from the Kingdom; with us always.

And the Holy Spirit shall recollect things necessary to quicken in your spirit, keeping you on the right path.

Expel foolish religious doctrines and traditions that lie, and falsify God's original precepts. His laws have NEVER changed.

Yeshua/Jesus advised us "I didn't change the law, contrary - the law is still in full force; and I am re-enforcing this understanding".

Father's keep your family in the presence of God (EDEN), which would cause for a healthy Society/Nation; for Our Heavenly Father.

And finally, God has given us (Man); a Beautiful Earth. An Exceptionally Beautiful Earth to have Dominion over. We must always possess a spirit of Gratitude and Thankfulness, to our Heavenly Father. He is so Wonderful, for this is Our

(Son's)Earth; Forever. And he will come down and dwell amongst us, from time to time, and will restore (make better than before) any areas needing attention (The New Jerusalem), yet; his dwelling is in Heaven.

This Earth is for our Spirits (Son's) to inhabit Forever.

Alhamdulillah..

As the wonderfully old expression says
Another Great Day In Paradise.
So Well Said… And So Fitting..

Parents, talk to your child/children, and give them good instructions; for it is for their good and safety (protection). This too is how God is with us. That's why he gave us instructions, via our Constitution - the Bible.   Therefore, we are not to deviate from these instructions. Just as a parent gives guidance to a child, Our Heavenly Father has already given us guidance; through our Constitution. And this has never changed, yet; all the more is enforced.   For God's word has never changed - either.

Man on the other hand, has deviated hard from God's original precepts; forming religions.

Religion is purely man-made, in attempts to soften God's instructions. God didn't do that. For God's word never changes.

His instructions/precepts remain, in Full Force.

And many people claim they have no time to read their Constitution. Therefore, the solution; Audiobook.

Conclusion

Jesus/Yeshua became the Passover Lamb and died on the cross for us, to atone us (with his PURE BLOOD), of all that Adam lost, restoring man (The Believer); back to SONSHIP.

Therefore, never allow the adversary to grab your imagination, and steal your sense of hope; and expectations.

And on this note (of expectation), God Bless the former Slave, because he never gave up hope; though he was heavily oppressed.

And do not have a bad attitude of what's going on (in the natural), whenever you're under attack by the adversary, because it all works out; for your Good. God has it already (ALL) planned out, ahead of time. Though we don't comprehend it (at the moment), God has it all planned out; to work in your benefit. For the adversary only attacks, when he knows there's something of value; going on with you.

Our Heavenly Father had to give up his son (Yeshua), in order to get his family back (us) as Sons, and Kings; underneath the Most High.

FEDDOR

And be mindful, we as Sons must often take
Communion - independently; freely in our own
homes. As it is instructed in ICorinthians 11 23-26,
do this in remembrance of all that Jesus has done,
to restore us BACK; to all of what Adam LOST.
For Adam fell from Dominion. And Jesus/Yeshua
came in the flesh. Our Heavenly Father came
down from Heaven in the flesh, and restored us
back to Dominion (those of US who are SON's -
Believers), and to all of our rightful and entitled
Inheritance & Benefits (as Son's), according to our
Constitution - via the Kingdom, upon this
Colonized territory here on Earth, that OUR
Heavenly Father yields to us and for our Spirits - to
Inhabit; FOREVER.....
AMEN....

Made in the USA
Middletown, DE
28 June 2023

33981997R00102